BOGIES

AND OTHER EQUALLY MESSED UP TALES OF LOVE, LUST, DRUGS AND GRANDAD PORN

RYAN BRACHA

Also by Ryan Bracha:

Strangers Are Just Friends You Haven't Killed Yet

Tomorrow's Chip Paper

The Banjo String Snapped but the Band Played on

Some of the stories featured within this collection have been available as standalone shorts, and have now been placed together alongside several exclusive stories. The standalone shorts are no longer available separately, with the exception of the novella, The Banjo String Snapped but the Band Played on.

Contents

FOR REBECCA,

WHO JUST WISHES I WOULD WRITE
SOMETHING NORMAL FOR ONCE.

BARON CATASTROPHE AND THE
KING OF THE JACKALS

One

My neighbour is a fruit and vegetable seller on Barnsley market. I see him every day, except Tuesdays and Thursdays. He loads up his wares at about five in the morning. His big white van rocking from side to side in the glow of the streetlights as he puts another crate into the back. It's the usual stuff; carrots, apples, cabbages, oranges, cauliflowers, peas in pods, tomatoes, bananas, strawberries, pears. From my bedroom window it's like he's just putting boxes of colours in there. A box of orange, a box of red, a box of green, a box of yellow, a box of white. Then he starts again, filling up his van with colours. Fruit and vegetables only ever seem to be those five colours. Or brown if it's gone off. Sometimes I can smell the awful tang of rotten fruit wafting over the wall, and I think that if I can smell it from there his house must stink on the inside. I don't know if I would ever want to be trapped in there. I bet there are flies. I don't like flies. Flies make me itch.

I wake up at a quarter to five every morning, except Tuesdays and Thursdays, and I go to my window to watch him load up his van. He's never seen me, at least I don't think he's seen me. I'm good at hiding. He takes about thirty minutes to finish with the crates of colours, and then he goes inside his house for between five and six minutes. I don't know what he's doing in there. I once took a glass to the dividing wall between our houses to try to listen to what he was doing but it was just the sound of shuffling, and when I got back upstairs he was closing the doors of his big white van and ready for driving away. It messed with my head for the rest of the day. I couldn't do anything right. Now I stay by the window, in the shadows.

It's when he goes into the house for between five and six minutes that I'm waiting for, because I know he'll come outside with *them.* They make me itch. I need to fix *them*. But I don't know how I can fix them. He's bigger than me so I'm scared to talk to him. I need to tell him to fix them. But then if I tell him to fix them then he might think that I think I'm better than him too. I don't know what to do. I hear his front door click shut, and the jangle of his keys as he locks it. The edge of the top of his head comes into view, he's nearly there, with *them.* Even from this distance and in the artificial glow of the orange streetlights I can see *them*. My fingertips start to itch, and it slowly creeps up my arms. The nails on my thumbs rub the insides of all of my fingers, but the itch doesn't stop. I'm clenching my fists to stop it but still it's incessant. My right shoulder begins to twitch, moving forward and backwards of its own accord. It's at this point that I sometimes need to move back, further behind the curtain, because he'll see me, but not too far. I need to see them, however much it makes me itch. I can't help myself.

Potato's 99p a pound, Strawberry's 80p a punnet, Califlour's 49p each, Bag,s of apple,s £1 each...

It goes on and on and on, and I feel my teeth grinding together. They make me angry.

POTATOES! STRAWBERRIES! CAULIFLOWERS! BAGS! APPLES!!

Carratts 99p a pound, bag's Of peas 90p, six Tomatoe,s 60p...

This is his *business,* how does he not know what he is doing wrong?

CARROTS! BAGS OF PEAS! LOWER CASE LETTER O! TOMATOES!

I don't understand it. It makes me itch. I know I shouldn't be watching it, but I have to. He puts the signs into the back of his big white van, on top of the orange, and white, and green, and yellow, and red. He slams his door closed with no thought for everybody else on our street, and he takes *them* away from my sight. I want to change them. I don't know how but I *have* to change them. I can't possibly be the only one who sees it. Somebody else *must* see it. His van turns the corner at the end of the street, out of my life for another day, and the itch doesn't subside, it gets worse. I scratch at a scabbed wound at the top of my arm, pulling the crust away from the skin and I gasp at the sudden pain, but still I scratch at it. It's dark in my bedroom but I can see the clear liquid seeping from the wound, twinkling against the lights outside. I scratch at the same place on my other arm until I draw blood. It takes about thirty to thirty five minutes to subside, and when it does I go to take a shower, and wash away the blood from the wounds I have created, and I get dressed in my bedroom as the light of dawn begins to filter into my bedroom window. This is what happens on five days a week of my life. I cannot change it. It's my obsession, my routine, my life. The worst thing about it, is that my next door neighbour, for all of the grammatical errors that he inflicts upon my existence, is just the beginning.

***

I like the number forty four bus at this time of day. All of the children have gone to school, the people have gone to work, and the roads are clear. The only time it stops is at the traffic lights, or sometimes at bus stops. Familiar faces appear now and then, offering thin smiles and token pleasantries. The woman I like to call Mrs Greencoat. I don't call her that to her face. She gets on the bus on Park Road, near the fish and chip shop, and offers me a small acknowledgement. She wears a green coat no matter what the weather is, it's the same kind of green as chocolate lime hard sweets. She wears a brown skirt that comes to just below her knees, and there's the grey-purple band of flesh of her legs before some pale stockings bite into the skin halfway up her shins. I don't know what those stockings do, but I see a lot of old people wearing them. I make my mind up to ask my mother when I see her next what they're for. The bus rolls up the hill toward the church at the top of the road. At the traffic lights I see a bald man wearing a black leather jacket knocking loudly on a white door, his knocks seem borne of anger. I can't hear him but he is shouting into the house, as if he was the big bad wolf and his anger could huff and puff and blow the door down. A woman appears at the window and shouts back at him. I accidentally catch her eye, and the man follows her line of vision to look at me. I feel myself go all warm and red when they catch me looking, and now I'm the object of his aggression. Again it's muffled so I don't know what he's saying to me but it's probably swearing. I don't like swearing. Thankfully the lights change and the bus moves around the corner, up toward the eyesore that is pub which has closed down and been abandoned. Its face is tattooed with the graffiti. It's been the same for years. A lot of pubs have begun to close down. I read that somewhere. I like to read. The bus slows again beside the abandoned pub and The Slug Man slithers aboard. He smells bad, like he's never washed his clothes, and smokes in a confined space whilst wearing them, he goes out in his slippers, and just doesn't shut up. He speaks to everybody as if they're his best friend and it slightly unnerves me.

"Nah then!" he bellows gruffly at Mrs Greencoat who slow blinks at him once, then twice, before she eventually smiles and greets him quietly. The Slug Man seats himself directly across from Mrs Greencoat and sniffs up loudly, and I can hear the noise of resistance to begin with and then the slimy *whoosh!* as he dislodges the mucus in his nasal passage. I think he smokes too much.

"Cold innit?!" he says, very loudly. She smiles and nods.

"Electric blanket weather! I were tellin' our Sharon! Electric blanket weather! We should be wearin' electric blankets!" he laughs, I don't want to be listening but it's impossible not to. Walking around wearing electric blankets is neither possible, nor would it be safe even if it *were* possible. My tongue flicks against my top teeth inside my closed mouth. I need to say something.

"You can't wear electric blankets outside," I say, but he doesn't hear me, or if he does he's ignoring me, and is already talking about something else.

"Yer see Barnsley score las' neet?" he asks her, and she's shaking her head.

"Two nil! I tell thee it were magic! Two ruddy great goals! Goowin' up this season am tellin' thi!" he shifts with agitation or excitement or something in his seat, and his face alights with the same emotion. She turns her head to watch the green field on the right, like she's had enough of being polite to him, and he continues muttering things to himself.

       The bus continues through the small estates and across Dodworth Road, and as we enter Pogmoor he's there. The King of the Jackals. He's the closest thing to a friend that I have. He's the only person that I talk to properly. We make small conversations in the five minutes that we spend together every day. He's about my age, but doesn't dress as nicely as me. He's worn the same training shoes for as long as I've known him, and he has a small rotation of similar tracksuits. All of the same style, but varying colour schemes. His wispy grey hair floats, almost ethereal, above his skull. His face is almost horse-like. He's not a good looking man. He speaks in a broad Barnsley accent, but I find it useful to have him around. I'm learning to understand the dialect. I don't know his real name, but I do know that he goes to town early in the morning, and will visit bargain shops, looking for items that have been reduced to clear. He'll spend hours in Asda supermarket, walking the aisles searching for items with a yellow sticker. But it's not just the yellow sticker he needs, if it's been reduced once, he knows that if he continues to stalk the aisles it will be reduced again. He boasts of things that should be four or five pounds being reduced to nine pence. He says he can buy a three course meal for less than fifty pence. I have to admire his tenacity. I call him the King of the Jackals because I've seen his type of person before. They stand in front of the section at any supermarket where they put all of the fresh food that's going out of date that same day, creating an impenetrable human wall. I call them jackals. They rip the bargains from the hands of whichever poor soul has been tasked with issuing the *Oops!* stickers, like jackals would tear the flesh from the carcass of a newly hunted zebra. Based on his stories of adventures past, in my eyes he is the King of the Jackals.

"Hiya," he mutters to me as he takes his place beside me on the seat. I don't smile but I repeat his greeting. His trademark carrier bag swings between his legs as he grips the handle with both hands.

"How are you?" I ask, it can't hurt to be pleasant.

"Not bad, not bad," he says to me, "thee?"

"I can't complain," I lie. The scab on my arm hurts a little bit, but I don't want to talk about that.

"Where're tha goowin'?" asks the King of the Jackals. He knows where I'm going. I'm going where I *always* go.

"My mother's. She's ill. Flu."

She has a cold. His face creases in concern, so I continue, "She'll live."

His cheeks puff out in relief.

"Oh, that's good. Me nana deed last year frum flu. Or worrit pneumonia? Anyway, she were reyt as rain one day then she deed the next." His hand works as if it's a tree, tumbling in a rapidly diminishing rain forest. His nana, dropping dead. I wish I'd not said anything.

"Where are you going?" I ask, as if I didn't know.

"Morrison's. Av 'ad me eye on a range o' chicken meals, they go off today, usually three fifty! Reckon I can get 'em for fotty pence!" His eyes are wide, he really knows his stuff.

"Excellent. Any other plans?"

"Not really no, al probly just hang around theeya, see if there's owt else goin'," he shakes his head.

This is how these exchanges go, almost without fail. It's not so bad. It keeps me in human interaction. The hospital appears on the left, and as we pass it I ping the bell, and ready myself for leaving.

"Say eyup to thi mam for me!" he says enthusiastically as he shifts his knees to allow me to get out from the seat.

"I will. Goodbye," I respond, edging toward the front of the bus.

"Cheerio!" he calls after me. I'll see him tomorrow. The bus pulls away and he raises a hand to wave me off. I don't wave back but attempt a responsive smile. I walk toward my mother's street, and on the first lamp post I see there's a piece of cardboard tied to it with string. The cardboard is a poster. I wouldn't usually pay too much attention to it but I've seen it now, and I can feel my fingers curl involuntarily, tightening into a fist, and my arms itch. My breathing becomes shallow as I absorb the information upon it. *Funbury's Travelling Circus! Locke Park, Bank Holiday Weekend May 4th-7th 2013.* It's now June. The top of my right shoe pulls up almost of its own accord and scratches the itch on the back of my left leg. It won't stop. There's none of the usual comfort that scratching would bring, it just burns deeper. My throat constricts and I have to turn and walk away before I vomit. The poster has created a force field of wrong, and I can't pass it.

The arrogance of Funbury's Travelling Circus has now put an extra twenty minutes on my journey.

***

"So how are you?" I sit on the sofa. It's the flowery pale brown one that she's had since I was a child. There's still the dark, but faded outline of a stain from times gone by. I always avoid it. I know what caused it. The needles clack together as she knits another scarf. This one looks like it's going to be green and blue. She knits them and then she sends them straight to the charity shop. She doesn't send them to just a single one, she rotates the causes for each one. Cancer, animals, heart attacks, famine, blindness, she doesn't discriminate. Every charity shop in Barnsley has at least ten of her scarves, and there are *a lot* of charity shops in Barnsley.

"Same as yesterday, you?" she doesn't look up, her focus is on the blur of plastic and wool.

"Can't complain," I lie for the second time today. My heart is still thumping from a combination of *that poster,* and the extra twenty or so minutes of uphill walking that it has forced me into and I could throw up all over her. She seems happy with my response though, and we each sit in silence. The intermittent clicks and clacks of her knitting save us from total dead air. She has a television but I'm not sure she has ever watched it. Not least while I've been in the room with her anyhow. This is one of the things that we have in common. My fingertips rub the fabric on the sofa backward and forward. I used to write my name in it by pulling the grain of the fur back against itself.

"What do you call those little stockings?" I ask eventually, the question having been on my tongue for a while. Still her eyes remain upon her handiwork.

"What stockings?"
"Those ones that only go halfway up your shins?"
"Support socks. Or pop socks, I suppose"
"Oh."
Another mystery of my life solved. Another piece of my knowledge jigsaw clipped into place. Another reason to sleep somewhat better tonight.
"Do you want a cup of tea?" I ask. She responds to the affirmative by way of a low hum.

      I move through to her kitchen, which is as much of a throwback to my childhood as the sitting room. The brown roller blind remains at half-mast above the sink. Patterned glass chopping boards cover almost every inch of the wooden surfaces. The place is immaculate. The gas ignites on the hob and goes to work on the iron kettle that sits above it, and whilst I wait I count the tiles along the kitchen wall. I already know that there are ninety six. Sometimes I only count ninety four or ninety five, and panic that I've been wrong all this time. I hate being wrong. The kettle takes about four minutes to boil, and it's then that I start to construct the drinks. The cups are placed out first, and I fill them with hot water, before I drop the tea bags in and watch the pattern of the chemical reaction. It fascinates me. Once the water is a nice shade of brown I place a level teaspoon of white sugar into the concoction, and dilute them with milk. Mother likes to recycle teabags, so they are placed upon a dirty brown mountain of teabags past, which she will use two at a time when she is alone. I can't use a teabag more than once. The thought alone makes me itch.
"Who's having that scarf?" I ask as I return to the sitting room holding two cups, one of which is placed carefully on the cream coaster beside mother.

"Hospice," she replies, as much a person of few words as I am.

"Oh."

Clackclackclackclackclack.

"How are you for money?" she asks. She always asks. Money is fine. Money is always fine. I don't get a great deal, but in fairness I don't *do* a great deal.

"Well, barring a catastrophe I think I'll be okay mother. My benefits will be in the bank the day after tomorrow."

"Who's Baron Catastrophe?" she asks, absent-mindedly. If she's being funny or she wasn't listening I'm not sure. I don't say anything. Her eyebrows raise and a light smirk shines across her face.

"Get a sense of humour you wally, I'm pulling your leg," she smiles, her eyes detached from her handiwork for the first time since I arrived, and shining in my direction.

"Oh," I say, forcing a thin polite smile.

The scene plays out in much the same vein for another hour, and eventually I make my excuses and leave, but not before washing our tea cups and placing them back into the cupboard. I try to make mother's life as simple as possible. My walk back to the bus stop is hindered by my knowledge of the poster for the circus, and as a result I turn the corner to witness the back of my bus home as it goes up Summer Lane. I could start walking, to save my thirty minute wait for the next one, but I'd rather not.

Two

The heavy rattle of the roller shutter clanked as he pushed it up into its housing above the entrance to the shop. He loved that noise. It was the sound of the future. The sound of possibility. A deep, heavy, metallic clank of success. That's how he saw it. Beyond the front window he could survey all that was his. He extracted the keys from his pocket and rattled them around, another noise he wasn't sure he'd ever get used to, or bored of. The master key slipped into the brand new Yale lock as smooth as silk, and before twisting it he embraced the emotion it stirred. Pride, anticipation, excitement. The door swung open to allow him into the mouth of the building. The place smelled clean, and new. The terracotta tiled floor evolved into a pure white MDF counter with a face of smooth glass. Behind that face there were three just as smooth shelves, each awaiting the opportunity to take the weight of his wares. The fridges buzzed in the background, one crammed with soft drinks, bottled water, and the obligatory pint of milk. The other was chock-a-block with heavy Tupperware tubs filled with the sandwich fillings that he and Mary had lovingly prepared together last night. She'd done the mayonnaise based fillers, egg, tuna, cheese and onion, prawn. He'd gone to town and knocked some chicken fillers up, grated a couple of kilos of cheese, sliced the ham. It was good quality ham too, to Steve there was nothing worse than a slice of ham that had more water than it had actual meat.

He gazed lovingly up at the pricing board. It had been etched by his son Darren with one of those liquid chalk pens. Daz had always had nice handwriting, so it was natural that his skills would be called upon for that task. Steve thought his prices were competitive, but not so much that he'd drive himself out of business. People would always pay for quality, even in this day and age when everybody was skint, they would never begrudge paying an extra ten pence for a better standard of butty.

Over the last few weeks it never really felt real, it was always just a project that he and his family were working on together, a goal that they could work to as a unit. He'd never been as close to Darren as he had since they'd started. He'd always been a standard teenager, sulky and petulant, no worse than anybody else's kids, no better either. He'd spend most of his time either in his room or out playing football with his mates, they never really bonded. But whilst they created this thing together they'd chatted like mates for hours, and he'd gained some sort of respect in the family home from his son. Basically, this shop was the best thing to happen to them, and he was literally an hour from the beginning of a whole new chapter in his life. With this in mind Steve had a satisfied smile on his face as he wandered around the kitchen area. Lifting up the arm of the grill machine, he could almost smell the rashers of bacon that he'd be cooking up for the anticipated morning rush, and hear the sizzle of the sausages as he rolled them around for full coverage. The microwave would be serenading him with a low hum and then that tell-tale *ping* to tell him that the baked beans were ready to be thoughtfully smothered atop the rest of the ingredients of a BEST butty. Again Steve smiled, and then his mood increased further still when the rumble of the baker's wagon rolled up outside the window. *The last piece of the butty jigsaw.*

At six he opened the doors for business for the first time. That high pitched jangle of the door smacking against the metallic dangling bell above it, the satisfying *click* of the closed sign shutting off to make way for his more positive brother, Mr Open, and The Boo Radleys blaring out of the nineties specialist radio station on his retro style DAB, declaring that it was indeed a beautiful morning, all the sounds that made Steve feel like today was going to be a very good day. The customers began to filter through the door in drips and drabs, construction blokes coming straight from the van with orders of several breakfast sarnies for each of their colleagues. All very specific too, this was part of what Steve was looking forward to. A fried egg butty with brown sauce, but the egg needed to be well done because his mate didn't like a snotty egg, a sausage and bacon with tommy sauce, but the tommy needed to be squeezed onto the bread in a spiral because 'Bazza dunt like his meat dry', cue much sniggering between the blokes. Between these grown up kids there were actual kids, the schoolies popping in for bags of crisps to eat on the way to class, occasionally he'd have to reprimand them for swearing in his shop but they were generally well behaved. His was the only sandwich shop for at least a quarter of a mile, and by the way the first morning was going he had picked the right place at the right time, and he was buzzing. The morning passed extremely quickly, any new activity that you enjoy might do that to your time, you could even say that time flew if you were having fun, and fun was what Steve was most *definitely* having.

***

The morning turned to afternoon and the fillings were running out. The egg mayo that Mary had thrown together had gone down a creamy treat and what remained of it would maybe cater for two butties, three at a push, if he was sparing with it. He'd kept the place spotless, wiping as he went, killing ninety nine point nine per cent of germs dead, no way on Earth would he risk the upset stomach of a potentially loyal customer. His business would die a death before it had even drawn a proper breath of life. The radio had shifted to a dancey little number about keeping warm, it was vaguely familiar and had Steve waggling his backside to the beat, whistling out of tune to the music, eventually the repetitive nature of the song ensured he was *in* tune and well aware of how the lyrics might go before the end.

"Swit swoo! Look at them buns."

Steve jumped with a start at the sudden interruption, he'd been so engrossed in his work that he'd not even noticed the door opening, and his wife slipping through into the shop. He mock held his heart and let his knees buckle, the universally accepted mime for being shit right up.

"Ah say! You nearly gimme a bleedin' heart attack!" he laughed as Mary approached the counter, her elbows drawing up to rest upon it.

"Chuff off yer joker," she said affectionately, "how's it going? You look like you've been havin' fun."

Steve nodded enthusiastically.

"Oh aye, it's been great, they can't get enough of yer egg mayo lass, it must be that secret ingredient," he winked with a leer, he wasn't even sure what he was talking about himself, but the innuendo wasn't lost on his wife, who rocked back on her feet and hooted a sleazy laugh.

"Chuff off yer dirty little Herbert! Nowt in there but a bit of salad cream, you *can't* have egg mayo wi' out a blob of salad cream, gives it it's tang!"

"I'll give you some tang!" Steve grinned, grabbing a hold of as much of the meat in the front of his trousers and thrusting toward his wife, who shook her head.

"That's enough now you randy bastard."

Considering himself told Steve released his grip from his manhood, and approached his wife.

"No, it's been great love, seriously, they've gone mad for it," he said, the feeling of satisfaction coursing through his body, and defined the anybody that might wish to gaze his way by the look on his face, "I've got a really good feeling about it, really."

Steve placed his hand upon that of Mary's, before leaning over the counter to plant his lips on hers.

"Good, well I'm-"

Jingle jingle.

Another customer interrupted Mary by entering the shop. The pair of them turned to face the newcomer. The man which stood before them was adorned from head to toe in brown. A kind of milk chocolate ensemble, from his jacket with padded elbows, past his polyester slacks, the bottom of which reached their end just above the top of his plain socks which were, of course, brown. Even if they weren't so on show beneath his trouser legs Steve still wouldn't have had to look to know that they were also a delightful shade of chocolate. He didn't move, just stared at the pair of them, until a strange, and quite uncomfortable air arose around the trio in the shop. Mary looked to her husband, who returned the gaze, before they both looked back to the man. The eyes on the front of his balding, way-too-skinny head twitched sporadically.

"Can I help you pal?" said Steve. The man still didn't say anything, but his hand reached up to his opposite forearm and began to scratch at the material of his coat, his face visibly winced at the contact that he'd made. He was obviously a weirdo. Still he said nothing.

"What can I do for yer?" he asked again, and the man slowly responded, the arm that was doing the scratching began to rise, pointing to something over his shoulder.

"The sign," he said, "it's wrong."

"What?"

"You need to change it, it makes me itch."

"What the bloody hell are you on about?"

"Your sign, it's wrong."

"yeah, you said, but what the-" Steve stopped himself, this was *his* shop, that much was true, but he didn't want to curse in front of his wife, not in here anyway, "what the bloody hell do you want?" he repeated.

"What do you want?" Mary parroted from her side of the counter, her hand instinctively sliding to her hip, the elbow crooked.

"You need to change your sign."

"It's *my* bloody sign!"

"It's wrong."

"What the chuffin' hell is wrong with the chuffin' sign? Are you mental or what?" Steve had begun to lose his patience with the tennis-like conversation that they were having, which it seemed to only consist of the word *sign*. He slammed his flat hand down onto the glass counter, the sound of which reverberated around the empty shop. The man flinched, but his feet remained stuck fast to where they stood. His pointed hand drew back down though, and returned to its place of scratching at the arm.

"It's Arnie, apostrophe, *then* the letter S, then sarnies, no apostrophe, an E before the S. Your sign is wrong."

Three

I don't know *why* he doesn't understand what I'm saying. It's simple English. It's just punctuation. You would think that the man that made the sign would have *known.* Why did he not tell Arnie here that he had spelled it wrong. That the apostrophes were all wrong. He's looking at me as if *I'm* the one who made the sign wrong. I'm only here to inform him, but from his response I'm wishing that I hadn't. I couldn't help myself. I'd sat upon the bus and seen the sign from the road. I'd never seen it before. The shop must be new. It was the proverbial straw that had broken the camel's back. Before I knew it I was standing in front of the building, the sign, it made me *itch.* I scratched further at the wound that I have created, it has become very sore. I entered his shop and here I am. Arnie has started coming from behind the counter. "Arnie," I say, my hands now up, palms toward him, "you need to change your sign."
He stops, an exasperated look on his face, now he knows how *I* feel.
"My name's Steve, Steve Arneson. Who the," he pauses, and looks at the woman who stands beside him, "who the fuck are you?"
Who am I? I'm nobody. Just a man who hates bad grammar, and misplaced punctuation, and people who leave their advertisements up way beyond the date of the event that they are advertising. They are rules, simple rules, they are order. Order is good. This, is not good. My back begins to itch, it burns through my skin, into my muscles, my kidneys. I can feel the skin dancing beneath my clothes, ticking and pulling around each individual itch. I feel sick. I will *not* tell this man my name, I will not allow him that information.

"I'm Baron Catastrophe," I say. I don't know why I said that, Baron Catastrophe is a stupid stupid name, but I've said it now, "I'm Baron Catastrophe."

The man looks at the woman. The man is short, and his belly hangs over the belt line of his black and white chequered trousers. Those are chef's trousers. A man who makes sandwiches is *not* a chef. His dark, hairy arms have tattoos up and down them. One of them catches my eye.

"Your tattoo," I find myself saying, and he pauses to look at his arm, "it should be *till,* not apostrophe *til.*"

"You're windin' me up aren't you? Who chuffin' sent you?" he begins to laugh, and shake his head, his incredulity makes me itch further still. I can't stand it. The woman begins to laugh too, and now they're both laughing at me.

"Baron Catastrophe," laughs the man, Steve Arneson. Arnie, "you daft bastard."

"Don't laugh at me," I say, quietly, the itching burns deep, they continue to laugh, and I can't stand it, "don't laugh at me."

Their mocking grows louder, and each time the woman slaps a hand upon the counter it makes my eardrum buzz, and my skin itches more and more and more. I shouldn't have come here. I should have left the stupidity be, I should have let this idiot continue to advertise his ignorance. But I couldn't. I couldn't do it. Something had to be done. And now I'm saying it louder and louder.

"Don't laugh at me, don't laugh at me, don't laugh at me."

It's become an ever increasingly loud mantra but their laughter drowns it out.

"Don't laugh at me, you're the one who does not know how to use an apostrophe. It's simple English you idiot. You're the one who should be laughed at. Stop it. You're making me itch."

I make a grab for the woman, I need her to stop laughing, I feel so sick. I need them to understand. My hand reaches up to the woman's arms and I shake her. Suddenly the laughter is no more, the man is shouting at me, and the woman is screaming. Then everything goes loud, and there's this whistling in my ears, and I don't have a hold of the woman anymore, I don't have a hold on anything, not even gravity. I'm falling. I don't know what happened but another loud whistle ricochets through my brain as something hits my head. My eyes won't open but my ears work.

"Oh God, Steve, what have you done?"

"I hit him, he attacked you."

"Oh God Steve, I think you've killed him."

"I haven't, he's alive, he's got to be."

"There's blood everywhere, what are we gonna do?"

The woman begins to cry. A click. The door opens. Breathing. More crying. The heavy, grating anguished roar of the shutters outside coming down. The clang of the bottom of the same shutter crashing into the concrete. The sounds begin to echo more as they reverberate against the enclosed windows. Another click. A key turning in the lock.

"Okay, what we gonna do?"

"I don't know Steven!" wails the woman. I don't know what is happening, I cannot move. The woman continues to snivel.

Suddenly I can feel hands on my legs. They wrap themselves around my ankles, place pressure on my joints as they begin to pull. All I can hear is the rustle of my clothes against the slate floor, occasionally a slight thud as my head rattles across the links between slabs. I'm comforted to feel that my skin no

longer itches. This is what it must feel like to *not* itch.
I don't like it. It's not *usual.* It's not *the norm.*
"What are you doing?"
"Shut up, just shut up will you? Help me undress him."
"Are you mental? I'm not doing that!"
"We need to get rid of his body! Help me to fucking undress him Mary!"
"What if he's not dead?"
"He's dead! Okay! He's fucking dead!"
The snivelling continues behind the counter. She sounds like she's on her knees, just because her crying seems protected by something between us. Steve Arneson pulls at my clothing. My favourite trousers. My coat. My head smacks against the floor as he removes my jumper. My favourite jumper. I feel the chill of the air that circulates around the floor, lower than the warm air of the kitchen. I'm naked. I'm naked. This should be making my skin itch.
"Steven, what have you done? What have you done?"
"Mary, let me think for Christ's sake!"
"What have you done?"
"I've got an idea."
The next sound I hear is a *shhhhhing* of metal being extracted from metal.
"What are you doing?"
"What I have to."

***

"Hiya love, what can I get you?" asked the exhausted Steve of the smiling girl before him, her eyes poring over the selection of fillings for her sandwich. They picked over each one individually. The egg mayonnaise, the chicken tikka, the seafood cocktail, the huge tub of grated cheese, they all looked so delicious.

"Mmmmmm, that looks nice, what is it?" she asked, gazing down upon the tub of sliced meat. Steve followed her line of sight, and struggled to hold down the contents of his stomach. Baron Catastrophe. He'd spent all night, and it was literally *all night,* not the all night that a student might declare that they'd spent doing their dissertation when they'd crashed out at midnight because they'd smoked just a little bit too much hash. All night, he'd spent, chopping up the body of the weirdo, cooking it, slicing it, spicing it. Turning it into an anywhere-near-palatable sandwich filler. There was no way he was going to jeopardise the future that, this time yesterday, looked so bright that it was almost blinding. Mary had cried herself dry, sat there rocking on her backside, but one of them had to stay strong, for the family.

"That's Baron Ham love," he said, "speciality, exclusive to the shop, I get it from my brother's farm just outside Doncaster. Do you want a taste?"

The girl nodded her head.

"Yeah, if you don't mind?"

"Nah, course not, got to make sure you're gonna enjoy it," he smiled, reaching down into the tub, pulling out a stringy piece of Baron Catastrophe, and passing it to the girl. She took a bite, pulling the whole piece into her mouth, chewing, her eyes closed in a show of pure pleasure, then opened, a twinkle ignited in them.

"Mmmmm, that's lovely," she purred, nodding her dainty little head, "I'll have that on a brown bap please."

Steve pulled some of the sliced man up from the tub, dropping it carefully on to the bread.

"Any sauce?"

The girl shook her head, *no.*
"No thank you," she said, "I can still taste it now, it's really, *unusual.*"
"Tell yer mates, only place in Barnsley you can get Baron Ham."
"I will, thank you," she said, before her face took on a whole other kind of vibe, "just one thing."
"Yes love?"
"Well, I don't wish to be rude but, well, your sign, up outside the shop, it's wrong."

GLASS HALF EMPTY

I sit in the corner of the pub. *My* corner. Old Terry snoozes into his big, round gut a metre or so up from me. In *his* corner. The room smells of cigarettes but nobody's smoking. It's the aroma that each of us drags in as we nip out into the cold every ten minutes to spark a ciggie up and suck the life out of it before returning to our respective glum. The smokey particles following us in on our invisible slipstreams, before swirling around the hazy heat of the pub and settling on any and every surface in the place. The radiators are up to full and it sucks the moisture out of my mouth every time I open it. I'm supposed to be seventy per cent water but right now I'm closer to thirty per cent. On the TV the three twenty at Haydock is running and my horse *Bobby's Boy* is three lengths ahead of the field. It's looking like easy money. He looks so strong compared to the rest. My eyes flicker toward Southern Keith at the bar who's also got money on this one. Southern Keith is from the Midlands, but moved down south some years ago. He moved back up here for work last year and has become an ever present fixture in the pub. He's usually really quite pleasant, but his mood swings sometimes set me on edge.

"Come on you dirty shit!" he growls, one hand gripped firmly around the handle of his Nottingham Forest tankard. White knuckles. *Bobby's Boy* continues to edge further from the rest and I allow a smile, just a small one, to creep onto my face. This wins and it's my rent paid this month. Victory from the jaws of eviction. An unlikely outcome, considering my luck of late, but not impossible. I can barely watch. It will only raise hopes higher than they deserve to be. Higher than they ever get. Southern Keith downs his pint of heavy and slams the tankard onto the bar, ejecting Old Terry straight from his slumber, and attracting a raised eyebrow from Northern Keith, the landlord. Northern Keith was only called Keith until Southern Keith arrived, and we needed some way to differentiate. Old Terry mutters something. Smacks his dry lips together. Pulls the ale to his face and slurps hard on the tarry brown liquid. His head lowers again. Chin snuggling against his chest as if trying to find the most comfortable spot. "Calm yourself," warns Northern Keith. I watch as Southern Keith wipes the froth from his ginger beard and venomously eyeballs the landlord. Says nothing but slides his Nottingham Forest tankard across the bar and nods. The landlord obliges and takes some coins from the pile beside it. Nothing more said. Simon Holt, the commentator, becomes more agitated as the end of the race draws near. *Bobby's Boy* up front, five lengths from *Plastic Fantastic,* the rest of the field drops further off. Three fences left. "Come on Plastic Fantastic!" Southern Keith roars, "you slow arsed farkin' nag! Get yer farkin' arse moved!"

So now it looks like it's me against Keith. My horse against his. I need this. I need this so bad. Southern Keith's better paid than I am. He owns his house. He drives. He goes on holiday. There are two fences left and I can smell a roof over my head for thirty one more glorious days. My own hand clamps onto the edge of the sticky table. I don't get as animated as the bearded ginger, more out of fear of facing his wrath than anything else, but believe me, I want this more than he does. I *need* this more than he does. *Bobby's Boy* approaches the last fence. *Come on, please, one fence.* I can't watch. My eyes squeeze shut and my ears await the thud of hooves against turf. An excited confirmation from Simon Holt that he has landed. *Anything.*

It doesn't come. Instead I'm treated to:

"Yesssssss, you farking beauty!" Southern Keith slams his hand over and over against the heavy wood of the bar as he roars in delight. My eyes open to see *Plastic Fantastic* romping home, and *Bobby's Boy* out of sight. Toppled at the last fence. Southern Keith laughs hard. His fist pumping the air as it squeezes tight around the coupon. He drains his tankard of heavy. Fat drops of ale splash from his mouth and onto his chest, leaving blobs of frothy residue on his jumper. He wipes the booze from his beard with the back of his sleeve and my heart sinks. I sigh. Reality smashes through my hope like a stone through glass. I'll probably have to phone our Karen. Ask. Beg. Grovel for a place to stay tonight. Work on a plan for the next few nights. I've no credit on my phone so I'll have to walk round. I look down at my growing beer belly and suppose that I could probably do with the exercise anyway. Old Terry shakes his head at the celebrating southerner, and drops his chin back to his chest. Arms crossed.

"What are the odds of that eh?!" asks Southern Keith of nobody in particular, "thought it was lost, you beauty!" he laughs again. In his own joy he fails to recognise the despair in my face. He nods to my table. Turns to Northern Keith, "His glass is half empty, get the boy anuvva drink."

He's not wrong. My glass *is* half empty, in more ways than one.

THE BAD DAY

Eddie

'Waa waa waa waa waa waa waa-'
Slam. Eddie's hand swings over, an upside down
pendulum, arcing through the air and onto the
snooze button of the digital radio alarm clock that
he's had beside his bed since nineteen ninety three.
Twenty years. The radio dial has been tuned in to the
local station for much the same period of time.
Eddie's got six minutes until the next deep, monotone
series of grating bleeps will sound out. After that he
has six minutes more. He knows this because it's how
almost every morning for the last twenty years has
occurred. Six eighteen the first alarm, snooze, six
twenty four the second alarm, snooze, six thirty, up.
Shower, dressed, toast, out by quarter past seven, the
depot by seven thirty, town by five to, first departure
at bang on eight. This is Eddie's life. His wife, Babs
will go about her day until she starts her part time
shifts at the amusement arcade that doubles up as a
tanning salon in the mid-afternoon until gone tea
time. This is what happens. Aside from holidays to
Skegvegas to the caravan in the first two weeks of
June every year and the last two of August. Until
today.
Eddie's pressed the snooze, but an itchy feeling at the

back of his mind won't allow him that comfort of dropping back off today. He doesn't remember getting to bed. Doesn't remember getting in the house. Flashbacks.

You might as well have shagged him right there you slag!

He rubs his eyes with tight fingers, picks at the crumbs in the corners. They were in the welfare club. Quiz night. Usual spot. Corner of the game room, watching the youngsters knocking some balls about, gambling a couple of quid on each game. They were loud but not over the top. Just having a good time. Eddie and Barbara were knocking back the jars, the usual Wednesday night. Him on the premium and her on lager and black.

You've never fancied me have yer?!

One kid, late teens, maybe early twenties, was cleaning up, taking on all comers. Swaggering around the table as if he owned the place. Started giving Babs the glad eye, right in front of Eddie. Acting the big man, then swinging a glance toward Babs to see if she was lapping it up. It didn't take long for her to pick up on his vibe. Started licking her lips. Dropping him a sly wink.

Yer old enough to be his fuckin' mother!

It had started to grind on every single one of Eddie's nerves like sandpaper. The conversation stopped between them. Eddie watched Babs watched the pool playing teenage lothario watched Babs right back. Eddie snapped. Threw the table over before he marched up to the kid and decked him. Left the pub. Babs screaming after him that he was an animal.

Get back in there and look after yer fuckin' fancy man yer fuckin' bitch!

Walked the streets. Found another hole to drink in. Knocked back the nips. Numbed the anger. Lost minutes. Hours. Woke up here.

Eddie swings his arm across to the other side of the bed without looking. It's empty. With laboured effort he drags himself up onto his elbows, blinks once, twice. Her side has remained untouched all night. *She'll be on the sofa,* he thinks to himself, *she'll come apologising before I go to work, just watch-*

"Waa waa waa waa waa waa waa waa waa-"

Slam. That's the second alarm. He's got six minutes until he needs to shower, but he knows that this morning he's going to need more than that before he's ready to haul his bones from his scratcher. Eddie rolls over onto his back, drawing an arm up and across his eyes to shield from the rising sun that's piercing through the cracks in the blinds. His body wants to sleep for longer, but he's never been late for a day's work in all of his life. The citizens of Barnsley rely on him to get around. To get to work. To hospital. To the shops. His eyes close.

"Waa waa waa waa waa waa waa waa waa-"

It's six thirty. His still drunk, aching body switches onto autopilot and he finds himself upright, heavy heels thud against the floorboards and his body manoeuvres toward the bathroom. Pulls at the bathroom light cord. Realises that it's already light enough in there and plinks it back off. He's barely aware of himself as he steps into the shower cubicle, his hand spins the tap, starts up the shower. The hot streams of water serve to slowly but surely chip away at the thick film of lethargy that coats him from head to toe. Gives him the illusion that he's feeling much more awake. He scrubs at his nooks and crannies with Babs' bright pink clown's wig loofah sponge, coated in thick minty shower gel, made with approximately eight thousand actual mint leaves. The mint in the gel leaves a tingle around his arsehole and under his armpits, and serves to further awaken his senses just ever so slightly. He switches off the shower. Stands beneath the dripping head and loosely, half-heartedly dries away the water and a few still remaining suds.

Pick on somebody your own size mister!

Steps back into the bedroom feeling slightly more awake. Drops his backside laboriously onto the bed after pulling two odd socks and a pair of boxers from the top drawer. His drawer. One of the socks is inside out but he doesn't notice.

You're a fuckin' thug Eddie!

The toaster clicks up too early. The toast is barely even golden, let alone the deep brown that he likes. Clicks it back down for another revolution. Curses the fact that he can never get it right in the first go. It springs back up and sits in its slot briefly before he remembers himself and pulls the rapidly cooling toast out with pinching fingers. Spreads the white spread across its crusty back, silently bemoans the fact that it's not melting in as much as he would like. Bites into a slice and approaches the door to the lounge. It's pushed closed. Babs will be asleep on the other side of the door.

You're scum!

Eddie makes a show of opening the door loudly, hopes to wake her up, coax an apology out of her before he sets about his day's work. The sofa is empty. Babs isn't there. The evidence is that she hasn't returned all night. Eddie frowns. Checks his phone. Nothing.

If you think I'm comin' home tonight you've got another think coming you bastard!

The clock reads seven thirteen. He needs to go.

You fuckin' animal!
The drive to work passes in a haze of insobriety.
Eddie acknowledges that he probably shouldn't be on
the road, but he has a job to do. He reaches into the
side panel of the door and self-consciously plops two
pieces of chewing gum into his mouth, chewing down
hard on it. Swallows it. Hopes that it will go some way
to disguising the whiskey smell that fills the car. He
feels entirely detached from his body. At the traffic
lights before the turn into the depot he pulls his
phone out again. Still nothing.
Just fuck off Barbara will yer!
"Now then Eddie, how's tricks pal? Look like you had
a good un last night," smiles Keith, the bearded ginger
bloke who drives the same route as Eddie used to do,
as they pass each other on the depot forecourt, Eddie
en route to his vehicle. Keith has been with the
company for only a few years. He's an aspiring
author, used to be a sales manager, now he's happier
behind the wheel of his bus. He used to travel the
world for his job but he gave it all up to travel the
estates, carting the elderly from A to B. Athersley to
Barnsley. Seems to prefer it. It gives him time with
the family.
"Alright Ginger?" croaks Eddie, through a pained grin,
purses his lips, "Yeah might've had a few too many
pops, it'll be reyt."
Keith shakes his head with a grin, and wanders off
toward the main building. Eddie approaches his bus
and clambers aboard. Sits behind the wheel. Through
the haze of the morning after the night before he
struggles to put his brain into gear before he can
think of putting the bus into gear. His hands look
through routes, and pricing sheets. Nothing that will
help him.
I don't ever want to see you again!

He slots the key into its hole, and pulls his mobile out one last time. Still nothing. Without thinking a second thought his fingers dash out a short message to Barbara. *Alrite?* And he places the phone back into his pocket. He sighs deeply and turns the ignition, pulling the bus out of the depot.

Fucking SLAAAAAAAAAAAAAG!

Eddie's bus is in the station, stand seven. A variety of people begin to form a queue in anticipation. Some schoolies, a girl in an Co-op uniform, a few elderly women. With a laboured resignation that today is a task which must be undertaken he pushes the button. Opens the door. The passengers filter aboard and he sets the thing into reverse. Pushes it into gear.

Bzzzzzzzzzzzz. A text. The bus shunts forward to the lights, which are on red. Eddie pulls out his phone to see what Babs has to say for herself, which grovelling words she'll opt to use. *I'm sorry Eddie, can I come home? I love you, please.* The text does not say this. The words which are formulated upon his screen say nothing like this. Eddie's mouth drops open of its own accord. *for a yung lad he were great in bed. its over eddie.* At this moment Eddie's world comes crashing down. Thirty years of marriage. Two children. Two grandchildren. A house. Two cars. Sixty holidays to Skegvegas. The dog. It all stands for nothing. It's been obliterated. No more. Dead.

HOOOOOOONNNNNKKKKKK!

He is jolted from his pain by the driver of the First Bus number twenty two. The lights have turned green. With a steadily increasing pain in his chest Eddie starts the bus out of the station and drives his number forty three bus up Eldon Street and on to its first journey of the day. Eldon Street passes by in a blur, the result of a god-awful combination of inebriation, tiredness, and heartache. *its over eddie.*

People stick out their arms to climb aboard the bus in the town centre but they are passed without thought. Eddie's number forty three leaves behind him a slew of angry, confused, dismayed people.

He passes the town hall, and its recently erected abomination of a sculpture, a giant rusted comb. It had caused a fair bit of controversy when it had first been knocked up, owing to the drunken imbeciles who had thought to climb the thing. Passed the library. Passed every single arm that thought to try to hail his vehicle. *it's over eddie.* Bells were pinged as the increasingly agitated passengers picked up on the driver's growing instability.

"Excuse me," says the girl in the Co-op uniform, Eddie says nothing. His fist tightens. Threatens to rip the hard foam padding from the metal frame of the wheel. In his mind's eye Eddie sees the young pool playing Casanova with his hands all over Barbara's body. His slimy smile. That wink.

"Excuse me," the girl repeats. Eddie's eyes remain upon the road. The bus almost knocks over a young girl pushing a second hand pram across the road as the green man informs her that it was clear to cross Summer Lane. The speeding bus narrowly avoids the attention of a police car descended toward the main road, and also goes inches from destroying the front end of a thirteen plate Fiesta. Eddie barely notices the gorgeous yet fearful ginger girl whose own reactions have saved her life. *its over eddie.* Eventually a moment of clarity strikes him, a brief respite for his passengers. The bus scrapes up against the kerb and the door opens. The Co-op girl is first off, pulling her arms into herself, exhaling a sigh of relief. She's already got her phone out, snapping pictures which will serve as evidence of the crazed lunatic that thought to hold them hostage, albeit very briefly. The

schoolies jump off, hurling a barrage of abuse
regarding how the fuck they are supposed to get to
school on time from here. The elderly ladies tut, and
sigh, shake their heads. Eddie doesn't care. He has
only one thing on his mind. Barbara. As the bus
leaves the bemused passengers by the side of the
road, and he is finally alone, Eddie begins to cry.

Joe

He stands in his dad's best suit. Record of
achievement under one arm and a nervous hand
shaking in his trouser pocket. His hair is
immaculately sheened over with Brylcreem. The
white oily stuff, not the hard setting green gloopy gel.
His dad's let him use the good razor too, to remove
any of the sporadic fuzzy dark patches that, until this
morning, resided on his face from where he's been
trying to grow a beard in order to get served at the
Commercial pub. There's a nurse beside him. She
looks tired, like she's here from the hospital on the
back of the night shift, her backside rests against the
double blue bar of the seat in the bus shelter. She
nonchalantly smokes a rolled up cigarette beneath a
Smoking is prohibited in this area sign, blowing out
her grey breath into the air around them. Without
realising he's doing it Joe curls up his nose and takes
a few small steps away from the girl. She notices him,
but has seen enough blood, shit, vomit, and death in
the last twelve hours to struggle to care less whether
this youth in the too-big-suit is offended by her
smoking habit. Joe taps his feet, the toes slapping
gently against the concrete in what, in his head, is the
beat to an Eminem track that he knows, but can't

quite remember the name of. He's had it in his head for the last three days, only the chorus though. Even then it's only two lines of the chorus. He hates it when this happens. His thoughts float out off into the ether and he's left with two lines of a song he barely knows running around the inner circumference of his skull like a musical motorcyclist negotiating a wall of death. Joe checks his watch. Eight eleven. The bus should be here by now. The interview is at eight thirty. He sighs, and glances at the girl. She looks his way and they exchange the briefest of eye contact, he wants to say something, ask her if the bus has passed already but he knows that this would be stupid. If it had passed then she would not be standing here with him, and besides, he's been here long before the bus should have been. She senses that he's about to speak so looks away. Blows the last of her smoke away and flicks the yellow tab end onto the road. Joe follows its arc and watches the tiny split second firework display of the impact of the orange embers upon the road, which disappear as the wind carry them off into Pogmoor. He's never had a job interview before. They tried to prepare him for them at school, during the careers advice sessions. Sat him down. Gave him potential questions and pitfalls that might arise, but he never took it seriously. How could he? There was some smooth faced twenty something trying to role play with him but there was always a distraction. His best mates Callum and Jordan doing stupid faces behind Mr Watson. *No, Mr Watson's my dad, call me Danny.* Behind Danny. No matter what they did at school it would never truly imitate what would happen in real life. There was never any pay off from taking the careers advice sessions seriously. Today there *is* a payoff. This is the difference between blagging money from his parents for another few months, and being able to *actually* pay his own way in life. His mum has already informed him that he'll be expected to front up some board. Two hundred a month. That seems reasonable. If he gets this job he'll be drawing *at least* six pounds an hour. Six pounds. It doesn't bear thinking about. He'll be in the Commercial every weekend, frittering away his own well earned money on Strongbow and pork scratchings. He'll be able to move up in the clothing world. Ralph Lauren polo shirts, Adidas sambas in four different colours, a season ticket at Oakwell. *That*, is what it's all about. The step from getting twenty quid a week pocket money, to two hundred quid a week that he will have earned himself. Then when he's eighteen and they have to pay him a proper wage, it'll go up even further. Joe smiles with this thought, and the gods seem to smile right back down on him as he sees the forty three approaching up Summer Lane.

"It's here," he says to the nurse, who lurches upright and begins to claw through her shoulder bag, retrieving her weekly bus pass. Joe's fingers curl around the two pound coin in his pocket, pulling it out and making a mental check that it is indeed a two pound coin, and that there won't be a hold up in his personal mission to get to Greggs in time for the interview. The bus rounds the corner onto Pogmoor Road and Joe's already got his arm out. From a distance the driver looks ugly, harassed, crying? The bus shows no sign of slowing for Joe or the nurse, instead seeming to speed up slightly as the bus driver, a bald scrunched up faced middle aged man, punches the accelerator in a show that he's got no intentions of letting the pair board. Joe's own features turn from fresh faced anticipation, joy at the bus arriving, through frowning confusion, into fear.

He shares a split second exchange of eye contact with the driver, and in him he sees fury, frustration, and desperation. But mostly tears.

"What?" asks Joe of the world around him as the forty three glides past him, arm still extended out of some bizarre hope that this is just a cruel joke and that the bus will slow. Reverse. Allow him on board. But no, it sails further up Pogmoor Road, rounds the bend, and disappears out of his life forever. He looks to the nurse, who looks back. Shrugs. Lights up another cigarette and slowly reverses, dropping her arse back onto the double blue bars of the shelter. Blowing out another stream of grey breath beneath the *Smoking is prohibited in this area* sign.

"I've got an interview in fifteen minutes," Joe says to her, his voice starting to ever so slightly show cracks, he wants to cry himself. The nurse shrugs once more. "Best get running then eh?" she offers, another arrow of carcinogens snaking from her lips. Joe ponders this. Watches the indifferent look in face as she turns away and watches the cars go by. He checks the time once more. He really does just have fifteen minutes. If he runs he *might* make it. He can explain what happened. The way the driver looked positively suicidal. That he'd been waiting for ages for the bus. But then a flashback hits him from Mr Watson, Danny's sessions. *Aim for the bus before the bus that you need. Be prepared for all eventualities. If it's going to be tight, book a taxi instead. There's no excuse for lateness. An employer knows this, and they will judge you on it.* As if his legs have got the message long before his brain has he's being carried quickly through the car park across from the hospital. He wants to cry. He really wants to burst into tears but he's a boy on a mission. His dad's smart shoes slap harshly against the pavement, the soles are far too smooth for this sort of endeavour. *Clack clack clack clack clack clack.* The bottom of his shirt comes loose, flicks up against his chest. *Thp thp thp thp thp thp.* His smoothly oiled hair flicks against the top of his head. He can hear it. *Tap tap tap tap tap tap tap.* Joe has never wanted anything more than this opportunity, ever. His back begins to sweat and he can feel the air circulate up his open shirt, cooling the beads as they roll down the base of his spine. Shaken loose of his pores by the jerking motion of his awkward run in his dad's best shoes. His young heart struggles to keep up with the effort he's putting in to get into town before eight thirty. He looks once more at his watch, eight nineteen. He's rounded the corner of Summer Lane and can see the beginnings of Barnsley town centre in the distance. Beside him the pubs and shops become a cartoon-like blur. In his tunnel vision all he can see is the town end roundabout. He's not much more than five minutes from Greggs. The Ralph Lauren polo shirts creep ever more toward reality. The Adidas Sambas in four different colours. The underage drinking. The board he can pay his mum. The season ticket at Oakwell. The new iPhone. It's all a possibility, Joe will simply *not* allow the crying, desperate bus driver to kill his dream. He's an Olympic athlete. He's Cristiano Ronaldo. He's even Justin fucking Bieber. All he has to do is negotiate Shambles Street and he's on the final stretch. He dodges the pedestrians with the nimble footed expertise of a champion boxer, and skips over the first lane, navigates the chicane of the traffic island, and steps out onto the second lane. The-

Danielle

She didn't see him. He just stepped out of nowhere. A young lad in a suit. All she did was briefly glance at her phone, a picture message from Pete. Him holding the cat. Then an almighty crash as the boy's legs buckled in front of the car's bumper. The speed she'd been going at was enough to flick him up onto the bonnet and over the roof. The car behind her driving straight into his prone body on the ground. Mangled him beneath its wheels.

He's dead. He *has* to be dead. Nobody could possibly withstand being hit twice. The kid is under the car behind her. Danielle slams on the anchors and waits. She knows what she's done. She was looking at her phone. In her rear-view mirror she sees the public screaming and wailing. Arms pointing to her. Pointing at the kid underneath the car behind. A dozen people reach into their pockets and handbags. Pull out mobile phones. Some are holding them up to video the carnage. Vultures. Others are jabbing fingers onto touchscreens. Pulling the machines to their ears. Phoning ambulances. The police. *Oh God, the police,* she thinks. She can't be arrested. She's only been working at the solicitors for three days. Christ, she's only been out of university for a couple of months. *This isn't happening, this isn't happening, this isn't-*

A pair of hands, and a face, slam up against her driver's side window. A woman. She's shouting, through a whiskered mouth, blackened teeth filling the orifice like bruised fingernails. Danielle has no idea what she's saying. The whiskers woman points back. Danielle cannot be sure whether the woman is angry. Blaming her. The wrinkled face seems to hold no ability to display anything other than a scowl. *The eyes.* In the eyes it's anger. She blames Danielle. Her shouting increases, and stringy spittle ejaculate spurts from her mouth, all over the window. Her face pushed up closer and closer. Fogging up the partition between them. Giving Danielle a short respite from those eyes. People are gathering around more and more. Rubberneckers. The entire customer base of KFC are out now, fingers point at her. She still cannot move. In the rear-view she sees that the man from the car behind is out of his vehicle. Head in hands. He's crying. A woman comforts him. Pulls him from the road and sits him on a wall. Another man has dragged the boy from under the car. He's giving CPR. *Ah ah ah ah stayin' alive.* Still Danielle is frozen. Her quivering lip, and darting, panicked eyes the only evidence that she is real. More people point. The man in the car couldn't help it. He's a victim. *She* is the one they'll blame. Dangerous driving, they'll say. Without proper care and attention, they'll accuse. Using a mobile telephone, will be the cry. Her job. She'll lose her job. The crowds grow further. Watching the man perform CPR. Watching her. The dented bonnet. The cracked windscreen. She did this. She is the one they'll hang for it. She panics. The foot presses firmly on to the accelerator and speeds her car away from the crowd. From the boy. From the man in the car behind. From her crime. The car spins around the roundabout, and onto West Way. She needs to find somewhere to go. Somewhere that they won't judge her. Pete's? No. Pete would call her a silly girl. Her parents will call the police. She continues her mantra, her lips flickering the words. Her face streaming with tears. *This isn't happening, this isn't happening, this isn't happening,* but it *is* happening, and it's happening to Danielle. Thankfully the lights are all green as she passes the Morrison's and heads up into the estate, past the old Gala Bingo and a quick left turn at the small roundabout, slowing to a halt as she creeps the Mondeo out of sight. Nobody around. She begins to cry. A heavy wailing. She notices a small spatter of blood around the epicentre of the crack in the windscreen. Where the boy's head must have made impact. *This isn't happening, this isn't happening, this isn't happening.* Maybe the boy survived. Maybe he's up on his feet, thanking the people around him. *Don't be fucking stupid. He's dead. You killed him.* Danielle drops her head to the steering wheel. Sobs uncontrollably. She's killed somebody. She's killed somebody and then driven away from the scene of the accident. She's going to prison. They're going to strip her of any dignity. Any respectability. *You've done it!* They're going to stand her up before the boy's parents. They're going to point the finger and they're going to judge. She's going to prison, for a very long time. When she comes out of prison she's going to come out to nothing. No job. No friends. Who would want to be friends with a murderer? A hit and run coward? She'll have no money. Her parents will disown her. *Who'll look after the horses?* She's ashamed to think this, but it's all up there, in her frazzled brain. She's going to prison, and the horses will be sold. To pay for her legal bills. Would the firm give her a discount? *You killed somebody you selfish bitch!* The house. Who would look after her house? How would it be paid for? *You took your eyes off the road and you killed somebody. You'll hang.* Facebook will condemn her. There will be a hundred groups in honour of the boy she killed. There will be a hundred more calling her a selfish, dangerous driving, hitting and running bitch. They'll hate her. All her life she's been so loved. So *popular.*

They'll strip her of that. *You're stripping yourself of it. Go to the police. Hand yourself in.* She owes the boy something. She has to show remorse. Maybe they'll reduce the sentence. Danielle brings her head up from the wheel. Wipes away the tears. A moment of clarity. She looks at herself in the mirror. Her stupid red eyes, her expensive makeup streaming down her face, her bleached blonde hair. Her pretty face. The reason she was always so popular with the boys. So much more pretty than the rest of the girls, that's what they said. *Go to the police.* She knows what she needs to do. She needs to get her own selfish head out of her own selfish arse and own up. Hold up her hands, apologise, show the remorse that they'll so desperately crave. Maybe they'll be lenient, maybe they'll see that it was an accident, he came out of nowhere, there was nothing she could do. *But you ran.* She can say she panicked. Didn't know what to do. Maybe now she's clearer of head she can walk into the station. Show them how sorry she is. Danielle starts up the car. Wipes away the tears once more. Turns the car around. Drives up toward Worsborough Common. Danielle has always been selfish, she knows this. She's got through life on her looks, taken advantage of situations where she could, she's not stupid, she *is* smart. She'll show them. She'll show them that she *can* take responsibility for her actions. Not pass the buck. Cowards pass the buck. Adults, real proper adults will always take responsibility for their actions. She's comforted by this thought, and feels more resolve in her decision. She can do this. She provide the justice for the boy that his family will so desperately need. Closure. She can feel like a hero. *Hero's a bit strong.* But the sentiment stands. She will hold her head high, and

say *Yes, I did something wrong, but I'm only human, we all make mistakes. Everybody makes mistakes.*
She drives further on, up onto Park Road, and turns right, back towards Pogmoor. With a heavy heart and a new found courage to stand up to what she has done, Danielle knows that she can makes this right. She *is* a good driver, but, again, everybody makes mistakes. She turns on the radio, the station is slightly off, so she fiddles the dial just slightly. It only makes it worse. She presses the scanner just slightly the other way, and takes her eyes off the road just enough to miss the fact that there is the speeding number forty three bus with a crying, bald middle aged driver who has absolutely no regard for anybody else on the road, and the front of his vehicle is heading directly for the front of hers.

Shaun

The pills should be working their way into his blood by now. The whiskey doing its job of assisting the process. But he can't be sure that he's taken enough. What if he simply passes out and wakes in a few hours with a banging headache? This is his fear right now. Not the end. No, he's made his peace with that. This is what he has to do. This will show her. This will make her see what a self-centred cow she has been. She took the kids the day before yesterday, packed them all up and off to her sister's. She's a bitch too. She didn't help. When Susan would have gone off telling her that they'd be arguing a lot recently, Mandy would have poured poison into her ears. Told her that they were all better off without him. That Susan was still young enough to find a man who would treat her like the princess that she is. The beautiful woman. An elegant woman. *Yeah right.* This was the kind of shit that Mandy was good at. Lying. Susan is as much to blame in all of this as Shaun is. She was the one who got caught sucking the reported kiddy fiddler Antony Bowen off behind the Warren pub. She was the one who drove Shaun to go out looking for an indiscretion of his own. If it weren't for her then he wouldn't have found a local scrubber to punish her with. The condom wouldn't have snapped. And they wouldn't have Lesley fucking Turner on their door step demanding child support before the rancid thing had even been born. It probably wasn't even Shaun's. Everybody knew what a slag Lesley Turner was. He said this to Susan, told her it was her fault, but no. The damage was done. She was taking Tyson and Bruno with her, and she was going to spend some time at Mandy's. The bitch. Shaun looks up at the light fitting. It looks strong. Besides, it only has to hold him long enough to do the job. He pulls a chair from the kitchen, places it beneath the light. Pulls at the cord. It seems strong enough. Around the cord he places the piece of the washing line he's cut from in the garden. Made a noose as best he can. Climbs down and takes another swig of economy whiskey from Aldi, a deep, gulping swig that burns his throat. On the mantelpiece there are pictures of them. The boys. Tyson and Bruno. He could fight for them but he has no fight left in him. He only wants to punish her. He's never been violent toward her. He has never once raised a hand to any of them. It was just one stupid idea after she'd made the first mistake. Now she's gone. The boys are gone. Shaun has every intention of being gone himself. He climbs back up to the light. Tugs again on the washing line. Ensures that it's stuck tight. There can't be any

mistakes here. They'll section him. This is why he's taking no chances. A belly full of Tramadol and a half litre of whiskey. The washing line above him. Ready to snuff his life out once and for all. Let that bitch see what she was missing, when she has to raise the lads by herself. He'll show her. He'll show her stupid sister. He'll show them all. Shaun takes one last sad look at the photographs. Happy times. Butlins last year. The week in Skegness. It was a great holiday. The smiles on the boys' faces breaks his heart but he's determined. He's resolved to do this and there's nothing that can stop-
CRASH!
Suddenly the world slows down, Shaun is holding the noose above his head, but cannot focus on this anymore as the back end of a Ford Mondeo comes smashing through the front window of the lounge. Glass shatters, bricks fly, the TV is flung across the length of the room. The sofa cracks in two and a cacophony of noise rings all around Shaun, standing in his *You're at the top of my to-do list* T-Shirt, and pissed in boxer shorts, atop a dinner chair, holding a green wiry length of washing line above his head. He does not move. Cannot move. The chaos unfolds around him. Through the newly created hole in the front of his house he sees the crumpled up front end of a Stagecoach bus, which has come to rest on the bit of grass in front of the chippy across the road. People running to assist the driver. Pulling him from the wreckage. The man from the corner shop is out and at the driver's side of the Mondeo. He pulls a blonde girl from the car. Lays her flat. He's performing CPR on her. People are all around the carnage. Across the road the driver of the bus is dazed. He's a bald man sitting on the grass, head in his hands. Mrs Juggins from across the road has brought a blue fleece

blanket out and has wrapped it around the bus driver. A crowd gather around the man from the corner shop pumping hard against the blonde girl's chest, holding her nose and forcing air into her lungs. Her small breasts rise. Then fall. Then he hammers on her chest some more. Still Shaun stands, unnoticed by anybody around the scene of the accident. He should be helping, but the Tramadol are taking a hold, he feels drowsy. He needs to focus. He needs to do what he started, and as the girl suddenly breaths again, her life saved by the man from the corner shop, her feet jerk upwards, like in the films. Shaun quietly, and sadly blows one last kiss to the photographs on the mantle, lowers the noose around his neck, and kicks the chair away. Nobody notices, and as he slowly slips out of consciousness, his legs swinging from the ceiling, he acknowledges that it seems to have been a bad day for everybody.

PLAYING OUT CLOTHES

I'll always remember Playing Out Clothes. I met him
briefly in ninety two. I smelled him before I saw him,
really. That tangy, sweaty arse crack kind of smell.
Some sort of vinegar crossed with shit aroma, but
with a subtle hint of bread and butter. All wrapped up
in a bundle of clothes that, although washed, had
been left in the basket to collect a bitter damp smell.
Imagine that and you've got it. Now imagine that
stink sitting two chairs down in your very first high
school assembly on your very first day there. The
head teacher introducing herself to the new wave of
students, proffering words of well-meaning but
ultimately flawed advice on how to make the best of
your time at school. Words by somebody who had
clearly either forgotten their own time as a twelve to
sixteen year old, or simply misremembered it. Or was
just a blatant liar.

So I was sitting there, the words of advice floating out
into the room but struggling to mount any
considerable attack on my attention, which was
already well focused on one thing. That smell. Up, one
ahead of me and three to the right there was Colin,
my best friend from middle school but taken from me
when they put us all in classes. Colin was breathing
through his mouth. One hand clamped firmly over his
nose. I knew him well enough to know that he was

just itching to turn around and ask where that awful stink was coming from. Colin couldn't hold his own water. The absolute worst at keeping secrets. Always talking. Not always talking anything useful.
rarely talking anything useful. He was funny as hell though, that's why I liked him. One of our teachers once accused him of having *verbal diarrhoea.* We never really knew what it meant at the time, but we thought it was hilarious. I don't speak to Colin so much anymore. Sometimes we'll *like* things on each other's Facebook page. Jokes and stuff. That's about it. He's still quite funny.

That smell though, it was just the start. The head was dishing out her pearls of wisdom to ignorant ears, and suddenly there was things twitching in the corner of my eye. I looked down and Playing Out Clothes was repeating everything the head teacher was saying. Under his breath. His sweaty fists grappling with the legs of his fake England football shellsuit. Clenching and unclenching. Pulling bigger and bigger bunches into the fist. It wasn't in the corner of my eye by now as I was blatantly watching him. His lips muttering a whispered echo of the head teacher's words. His fists swallowing big bunches of shellsuit, making the left leg ride further up to reveal a sock. It might have been white once, but it was brown now. Not the kind of brown made by mud, like, the kind of grey-brown you get from soil. It was more a yellow-brown that you might get from shit. I couldn't help my lip from curling up in disgust, and then suddenly the clenching stopped, and Playing Out Clothes brushed the creased shell material out straight. I looked up and he was staring right at me. His brown eyes looking tiny behind the inch-thick glasses. I always assumed after that that his eyes must just be that small, because I never saw him without those glasses on. Honestly, they always looked marble-small. Smaller even. So Playing Out Clothes, he smiled at me and I didn't know where the hell to look, so I settled on the back of Julie Hamilton's head. The plait which ran tight from the purple scrunchy right down to her arse. Barry Schofield sat between us, breathing though his mouth. Trying not to taste the airborne germs that Playing Out Clothes would almost certainly be carrying. Just sitting down would send spores of filth in all directions. Barry's eyes were watering. I was close enough to Playing Out Clothes as it was but I couldn't imagine being almost on top of him. I wouldn't want to imagine it.

Still I could feel his beady stare in my direction. I ignored him for as long as I could, but he began to whisper for my attention. In the corner of my eye he was leaning further toward me. Across Barry Schofield.
"Oi," he whispered, "oi."
I ignored it.
"Kid," he whispered, "kid."
I ignored it.
"Your jumper's on inside out," he whispered. I looked down. It was. I was gutted. First day of big school and I had my jumper on inside out. Barry Schofield began to giggle. I turned and Playing Out Clothes was still beaming this gormless grin my way. I hated him for it. All he'd done was point something out, but you always shoot the messenger don't you?
"Yeah, well, you flippin' stink!" I cried out, drawing a gasped hush from the assembly hall, "my playing out clothes are better than your school clothes!"

You could've heard a pin drop, until Colin broke the silence, his trademark snorts of piggy laughter, even with a stern look from the head teacher he couldn't stop, his shoulders heaving in a wall of stillness, one ahead of me and three to the right.

"He does stink though," he laughed, "playing out clothes, brilliant. Classic."

Colin and I got a detention on our first day at school for that, and from then on in Playing Out Clothes carried two things with him everywhere he went; the smell and the moniker. I don't remember his real name. Last I heard he was a doctor though, or a surgeon. On an absolute fortune working down in London. Funny how things turn out isn't it?

BOGIES

As I peruse the shelf the weathered old shopkeeper, a thin and long stick insect of a man with a full head of white hair, gazes at me over the top of his specs like I've laid a heavy, steaming, long poo across the doorway like some ecologically friendly draught excluder. I don't know what his problem is, I mean, he sells the stuff, why judge the people that buy it? My eyes scan the titles beneath the *modesty sleeves.* Granny Sluts. Reader's Wives. Fifty and Filthy. Sixty and Sexy. Asian Babes. It's mostly niche stuff. I pick up Granny Sluts and turn to the counter, drop down the plastic coated publication with a heavy slap and a cheery grin.

"Alright?" I ask, with a smile in my eyes. The good gentleman vendor makes some gruff variation of a greeting. Scans the barcode with a bleep and doesn't say anything. Just nods toward the illuminated price which informs me that I'll be paying just under seven quid for this particular pleasure. Seems fair. I drop a tenner into his dry palm, slide the magazine into my leather satchel, and await my change. He eyes me suspiciously as he fingers the coins in the till, slowly bringing the change my way. Between the standard facial features there are long and deep wrinkles that it takes all of my resistance to hold from fingering curiously, just to see what he's holding in there.

"Thanks," I smile gratefully, not even a hint of shame in my eyes with the purchase I've just made. It's for the greater good. He'll love it.

I step out of the shop onto the busy street, dodging a young mum with a pushchair, kiddy screeching for something and nothing, I don't know. The mum seems stressed, venomously eyeballing the tot through the top of his or her skull, muttering empty threats. Her sunken eyes sit deep within blackened holes in her face. The hair scraped tightly into a greasy ponytail. Pulling her painted on eyebrows to far too northern a territory for them to look anything other than clownish. She's visibly wishing harm upon the little mite. I'd hazard a guess that she's as single as I am, except she chose to open her legs for the wrong man. My judgment stops there though, I'm not a parent, I don't know that I'd be any different to this girl with whom I have a fleeting contact. Maybe that's what parenthood does for people. Maybe she's a glimpse into a future that I cannot yet see. Probably not though, I think I'd be a good parent, I'm a good child, and grandchild after all.

***

"Hiya, is he awake?" I ask as I approach Fiona, the receptionist. She's pretty but not in any obvious way. You really have to look at her to see it. Her thick black hair is tied back tight into a pony tail, though not as tight as that of the world's best mum from the street earlier, and a lot cleaner. She has these big off white teeth that fill her mouth, the rest of her face hides behind big glasses that remind me of Deirdre from Coronation Street. When she stands up she's not fat as such, nor is she skinny. I suppose it's in the eye of the beholder and all that but for me I can see why somebody might find her attractive.

"Yeah he was last time I saw him, go on through," she says to me, pushing the door release to buzz me in. Immediately that smell hits me. That tangy smell of old people. My gran had it before she died, and now my granddad has it. So do all of his friends. I don't know where it comes from, I couldn't even say what the smell *is*, but it's not entirely unpleasant. It's kind of comforting, in an obvious way. I stride through the halls toward Granddad's room. I pass Mrs Doubtfire's chamber and she's in there sitting with a visitor. Not one I've seen before. Mrs Doubtfire isn't her real name but she looks like a bloke and has this soft Scottish accent. Calls everybody *Dearie.* She's alright. Not offensive in any obvious way but she probably hates black people behind closed doors. Her real name's actually Mrs McInally.

"Hiya dearie!" she coos from her chair, a slow arm jittering upright, her hand opening like an aged greying flower coming to bloom. I stop, partly because I don't mind indulging these people. I could be one of them one day. It's also partly because I like the look of Mrs Doubtfire's visitor. He smiles at me briefly but then as I smile back his eyes dart to the floor nervously and his face turns bright red. He's young. Ish. Younger than me anyway. Maybe nineteen. Cute. He's wearing a T-shirt with a snow tiger trying to rip its two-dimensional way out of his three-dimensional pigeon chest and tightly folded arms which sit atop his little belly. He's also got these too-blue denim jeans with the legs rolled up from where they're just slightly too long. Under that he's got plastic brown trainers with sticky Velcro instead of laces. Co-ordinated he is not. Charity shop fodder if ever I saw it.

"Hi," I say, my fingers picking at a sharp spot beneath the paintwork on the door frame as I stand on one foot and rub the back of my leg with the other. Mrs Doubtfire is smiling gormlessly and her visitor still scrutinises the floor as if scanning it desperately for a contact lens or the meaning of life. Or his balls. I decide to have a little fun with him.

"Hi I'm Sara," I say to him, willing his eyes back up to mine. I take a few steps into the room. He flashes a quick glance my way once again but it would appear that looking at me is the equivalent of looking directly at the sun on a scorching day. I hold out my hand, "what's your name handsome?"

So either his name is vomit or he's just a *very* shy boy because his next charming action is to throw up all over the shiny flooring, with a few creamy flecks making their way through the air onto my shoes. I frown.

"Delightful," I say, Mrs Doubtfire's still cluelessly waving and smiling and her visitor's looking up at me, glistening red eyeballs and slimy slathering chin which has started to quiver. *Don't cry.* His red eyeballs begin to distort beneath the blobs of water that are building up on the bottom lids. *Don't cry.* I turn and exit the room because I hate to see people cry. People in the street. People on telly. People in books. My mum at my Gran's funeral. I don't even like the whimpering of dogs. It breaks my heart.

The next open door goes into an empty room. It's where Mr Parker used to live. Now his room's empty. The bed all stripped down. Just an under sheet. The tops of the drawers and the windowsill are empty. Where there used to be trinkets and photographs. I get this awful feeling that Mr Parker's dead. Bless him. He was a good bloke. Funny. Sharp as a tack. When me and granddad used to sit in the communal lounge he always came over with these daft stories from his life. Some were obviously made up. They always started *Did you know I once...?* And then he'd go on to tell us how he once took Greta Garbo or Elizabeth Taylor to a dance when he was living in Paris, or how, when he was a professional wrestler, he was once knocked out and officially dead for ten minutes. Then when he'd finished his story he'd say with a cheeky wink, "No word of a lie," and then he'd turn his head, gaze off out of the window all sage-like, and suck his false teeth. Me and granddad would share this look between us. A look that laid somewhere between affection and *what the bloody hell is he on?* But we always humoured him. Such a shame. One of the good ones gone. I really hope he went peacefully. I don't know what I'm going to do when Granddad goes. I can't even bear to think about it. I don't make friends very easily, so he really is my best mate.

I press my face up to the crack of the door, one eye open and watching Granddad as he sits on the bed watching telly. From the nasal cartoonish tones emanating from the box I reckon he's watching *Dickinson's Real Deal.* The self-proclaimed Duke seems to be proffering some advice to an unknown character that's stumbled across a valuable rarity and is torn between the money on the table or gambling on taking the item to the next step. The auction room.

"Teck it to oction!" bellows Granddad.

"Now that is a very generous offer," says the king of all things cheap as chips, "but our *Oction Master* says it could fetch anything up to fifteen hundred pounds at oction, if the right buyer is there on the day."

"Teck it to oction!" Granddad shouts again, his hand slapping against the mattress. He gets ever so involved in what he's watching on telly sometimes. I feel a smile stretch my face a little. I love him to bits. "Well, you're right, it *is* a generous offer," replies the unknown person, "and the right person might not be there."

"Teck it to oction you bloody imbecile!" He's almost at the end of the bed now, another hesitation by the woman on telly and he'll be in there with her, ringing her neck.

There's a sudden movement in the corner of my eye as Mrs Doubtfire's visitor skips out from her room before he sees me and his outstretched arm grabs a hold of the door frame and he drags himself back into the room. It's almost comical. Bless him. With a quirky accordion soundtrack in my head I watch the doorway with amusement as his head then pops out, like one of those moles at the amusement arcade, before an invisible force of shyness bops him on the bonce and he's back in the room. This happens three times. I imagine Mrs Doubtfire is still sitting there, waving and smiling inanely. Granddad shouts at the screen again from through the crack in the door, and I turn my attention back to him.

"I'll teck it to oction thanks!" I whine through the crack, and a huge smile appears on Granddad's previously agitated face as he figures out who, what and where the voice came from.

"Nugget!" he roars in delight as I push the door open and walk through into his room, placing my bag onto leather chair beside his bed.

"Alright Henry?" I say, pulling him close to me and getting a great big Granddad hug. He smells of germoline. He won't let me call him Granddad to his face. It has to be Henry. Always Henry. It's been like that since I hit eighteen. He sat me down, told me I was a grown up, and if I was going to start acting like one that I should call him by his Sunday name. He called it that. His Sunday name. Bless him. He still calls me Nugget though.

"This chuffer here," he says, nodding toward the telly, "they've offered her eight hundred quid for this chuffin' necklace and she's wettin' herself over it, but *oction* master says it's worth a grand an' half." His face has taken on this wide open look of incredulity.

"I'd take it to *oction* me Henry," I nod sagely. It's funny, but since this telly show has been on neither me or Granddad can actually say *auction* anymore. It's always *oction*.

"It's a very kind offer, and I'd be delighted to accept," says the woman on the telly. She's got masses of brown curly hair and a great looking fleece jacket on, with a panda chewing down on some bamboo. I love the quirkiness of those jackets. The boldness of the people prepared to put their bodies inside them. The fact that anybody even thought to *make* them, let alone wear them.

Click.

Granddad's turned the telly off and he's shaking his head.

"Chuffin' idiot," he says, really disappointed. She's stolen at least five more minutes of entertainment from him.

"She is Henry; I don't know how she'll sleep tonight."

"Eight hundred quid," he mutters, "could've had twice that!"

I'm about to tell him again that I would've taken it to *oction* when suddenly the vomiting shy boy from Mrs Doubtfire's room is standing in the doorway. His chin is dry and he's doing his level best to bring his twinkling red eyes to mine. Granddad's watching him with some sort of expectation, as am I. He's kind of sweet but he's dropping sweetness points, and gaining creepy points for every second he's standing there saying nothing. Granddad looks at me, then back to the boy in the doorway.

"Can we help you sunshine?" he asks, his usual to-the-point self. He suffers fools for nobody does Henry. The boy looks like he's digging around in his brain for the words. Maybe he's found them but his mouth just doesn't know how to formulate them. His hands are burrowed deep into the pockets of his too-blue jeans. The insides of his elbow joints almost pointed outside they're twisting so hard. I giggle a nervous giggle and get up from Granddad's bed. The silence of no telly and the boy standing here saying nothing becomes deafening. Air whistles in and out of Granddad's nose. The soles of my trainers scratch quietly as they unstick themselves from the hard linoleum floor with each small step toward the door. An elderly woman wails in anguish from somewhere in the building. Still the boy says nothing and I'm right in front of him. I'm not saying anything either, lest I find the switch for another torrent of vomit all down my front. A few flecks on my shoes I can live with, but a whole gusher onto my boobs, well, that's another thing altogether. A nurse edges round us in the hallway and on to somewhere else. She's inadvertently shuffled us a few inches closer to one another and I'm looking at him expectantly. There's a strange lack of discomfort here. I don't know what it is but I really like the aura around the boy. Close up, when he's not being sick he has these really nice cheeks that sit quite high beneath his dark brown eyes. He's skinny but not frail. His dress sense is so ridiculously pitiful it's hard to believe it's not ironic. I just wish he'd say something.

"You're not boring," Granddad's voice echoes into the hall. I stifle a giggle and look over at him, telling him off with my eyes. I kind of like this silence now. There's something slightly magical about it. All I need is a string quartet to sit by us and provide some touching soundtrack. The boy clears his throat and eventually summons up the strength of character to finally meet my eyes with his.

"My name's Joe," he says, "I'm sorry I was sick on your shoes."

"That's okay," I smile, "it was only a little bit."

A soft appreciative smile wriggles onto his face and he fights again with himself to say something else. I wait expectantly.

"Have you got a boyfriend?"

A snort of laughter takes me by surprise. Granddad's been listening. I tell him off again with a playful scowl and a shake of the head. He turns his head as if he's not been listening, chin jutting to the sky.

"Uhm, no," I say, "not anymore."

I haven't had a boyfriend in ages, I don't think I could even consider any of the few men I've been intimate with to be what you might call boyfriends. Dalliances? Yes. Flings? Perhaps. Boyfriends? Probably not.

"Do you want to maybe come out with me one time?" he asks, his eyes are back in their usual spot on the floor. His hands still burrowing deeper and deeper into his pockets. He's not used to asking girls out. *No shit Sherlock.*

"Uhm, yeah why not," I nod, it can't hurt can it?

"Cool."

Then he stands saying nothing again. I don't know if he's thought out what would happen if I said yes so he's looking a bit lost.

"When? Where?" I ask, and he lets out this little laugh through his nose, and shakes his head.

"I don't know," he says, "I didn't think you'd say yeah."

"Why did you ask me out then?"

He shrugs.

"You're pretty."

I blush.

"Thanks."

"Nugget? Did you fetch me my mucky magazine?" calls Granddad from his room. I could kill him, he's a real wind up merchant. Joe's eyes widen. I feel moved to explain.

"He likes Granny Sluts, it's his favourite."

"Man's got needs!" shouts Granddad with a laugh.

"Henry behave!" I gasp, Joe doesn't know what to do or where to look. Bless him. "He just likes the pictures."

***

"So how comes you buy porno magazines for your granddad?" he asks. A fair question I think.

We're in a small café called Linda's, round the corner from Granddad's care home, and it's a couple of hours later. I like it. It's got a few people in but it's not too busy. The eponymous Linda has been and taken our orders. Joe's gone for a coffee and a sausage sandwich and I'm on diet lemonade and a cheese salad. This isn't a *date* date. No, I'm dressed far too shabby for that. No, this is a pre-date date. A bit of getting to know you and all that.

"It makes him happy," I say, before wrapping my lips around the striped yellow and white straw to slurp up a mouth of fizzy pop, and it does. There's nothing

more to it than that. Joe seems to ponder this, then he
nods, like he gets it.

"Okay, you next."

"Why did you throw up on my feet when I said hello?"

He thinks about it. Takes a drink of coffee. Puts his
cup down on the table. Smiles. A shy smile.

"Girls don't talk to me very often. Could you tell?"

I nod.

"You're very pretty."

"Thanks."

"Pretty girls talk to me even less often than just girls.
They think I'm weird."

"Do you kill small animals?"

"What? No!"

"Do you touch yourself inappropriately in public
places?"

"No."

"Why do they think you're weird?"

"You were only allowed one question."

"They're all extensions of the same question."

"No they're not."

"No, they're not. But I'm on a roll. Answer the
question."

He smiles and shakes his head. Sighs.

"I don't know. Maybe it's the way I dress."

"What's wrong with the way you dress?"

"Nothing as far as I'm concerned. Others disagree."

"Sod what others think."

He smiles again.

"My turn?"

"Sure."

Our sandwiches arrive and we continue in much the
same way, quick-fire questions and responses,
getting to know the small, daft things about one
another. Before we've finished eating I know that

Joe's favourite flavour of crisps is Prawn Cocktail. His favourite word is sponge. He prefers showers to baths. He ties his right shoe first all the time. He has a weird phobia of little stickers. Those small circles that they have on the inside of new clothes. Between us we decide that they're for quality control but neither of us could be sure. Whilst he's telling me about it I can see his hands bunch up, like they're itching at the thought of stickers all over them. Strange, but it's his thing. He's entitled to be fearful of whatever he wants. He says this is why he wears charity shop clothes. The quality control sticker will be long gone by the time it reaches him. Before the bill comes he knows that my favourite crisps are Beef and Onion. My favourite word is moist. I also prefer showers. I think they're just easier and quicker. Yes, there's a certain pleasure to be derived from a nice long soak but all in all it's about getting clean. I can lie on my bed and read a book if I want to relax. I don't tie my shoes at all. I like to tuck the laces down inside the shoes, or trainers, or whatever. It makes for an easier ejection of foot from footwear in case of an emergency. I say this to him and he laughs. Because he laughed I do a stupid impression of my foot as a pilot, pressing the ejector button and, complete with a *pshtoooooooo* I eject my foot, and even act like it's got a parachute attached, floating it back down to solid ground. I'm such a tool. He's laughing his backside off and I'm feeling good. We've got a really, really, *nice,* vibe between us. We get each other. I like it. I could *definitely* see him again. If he asks.

Before we leave I excuse myself and go to the toilet. In there I do my business and then stand smiling in the mirror. This isn't one of those clichéd times where I'm scrutinising every inch of my body in disgust. Far from it. I'm just smiling at myself because my reflection is the only person in there to share my glee with. Joe is really cool in an uncool way. Just my kind of boy. I'm not planning marriage and babies or anything. It's just that this is the first time I've actually *clicked* with a boy. Like, in an obvious way. I saw the way he was looking at me. He thinks I'm pretty. He said I was pretty. I pull out my phone and scroll down. I find Henry and I fire off a quick text. *It's been brilliant xxx.* He doesn't respond straight away. He never does. It took all of his patience to learn how to use the phone I bought for him. It's only a basic one. It texts and calls. That's all he needs. He said as much himself. It was more for me than anything else. Just to know that he knows he can get in touch with me at any time he wants. I wash my hands and have one last smile in the mirror before I skip out of the toilets to my waiting potential boyfriend.

We walk together. Talking some more. About music, and online games, and books and films. Thankfully he doesn't like football. I *hate* boys who like football. They get obsessed. Turn it into some sort of reason to argue and fight. Pledge allegiance to ten or eleven men who they've never met who play their games hundreds of miles away. They *never* go to watch a match but will happily fight to defend the honour of Manchester or Arsenal or Liverpool or any of those places. Idiots. We stop by the River Don and perch ourselves on a bench. Joe's hand rests on the wooden slat beside my leg. I can see the twitching thing willing itself to take some sort of leap of faith and plant down on my leg, or better still, to grab a hold of my hand. It doesn't happen.
"I like you, you know?" he says and my heart skips. I smile, but don't look at him.

"I like you too."

"Do you think-" He stops himself short. I turn to him. "What?"

"No, it's too soon, forget it," he says, shaking his head.

"No, what?" I've shifted my body to face him now. My knees touch his. My hand placed down upon the bench. My index finger just slightly brushes the tip of his little finger. It sends a tingle up my forearm. I like it.

"I just wondered."

"Spit it out!" I laugh. My hand has edged closer to his. His little finger rubs against me gently. I'm willing his hand onto mine.

"Can I kiss-"

We're kissing already, it was all I needed to pounce on him. To wrap my arms around his neck and push my lips hard against his. His arms flail slightly but then he finds his comfort zone and suddenly one of his hands is cupping the back of my skull, the other is rested on my waist. This kiss is phenomenal. When I woke up this morning I did *not* expect to be having a passionate kiss by the side of the river at some point today. I stifle a little giggle when Joe's willy presses against my leg. He's *very* turned on. I'm not that kind of girl though so I shift my leg back a little, out of range of his little torpedo. I don't want to encourage that. We've only just met after all. His tongue creeps out from between his lips and touches at mine. Just the tip. It feels nice. I open one of my eyes and I see that his are squeezed shut and he's really in to this. So am I. I close my eyes again and we kiss a little while longer. Eventually his tongue is exploring my mouth. Pushing deeper and deeper into my throat. I wrap my own tongue around it for every revolution and we could be anywhere right now, all we know is each other and-

We're ripped from our embrace by the high pitched yapping of a small dog. A Yorkshire Terrier. It's scurrying around our feet and we laugh. Our bubble has burst and reality floods into our lives once again. The owner is an old man in a dirty camel coat, and beneath that he's wearing pyjamas. It's only dinnertime. We go quiet and hold hands until the man and his dog pass us, and almost simultaneously burst out laughing.

"I want those pyjamas," says Joe.

"Nah, he looks like the kind of man who leaves the stickers in, you'll poo your pants," I laugh and Joe feigns hurt before slapping my leg.

"Cheeky," he says, and we go quiet. Joe absent-mindedly guides a finger to his nostril and begins to pick so I turn to watch the back of the camel coated pyjama man and wonder what his story is. In my head he's called Jack. John on a Sunday. His Sunday name. My mind then wanders to Granddad. I wonder if he'd approve of Joe. I'm sure he would. He's a really nice boy. He has the same silly ideas as me. He gets me. He thinks like I do. He's cute. He's a good kisser. Okay, so kissing good isn't at the top of Granddad's list of priorities for any potential boyfriends of mine, but still. His tongue was so eager. I'm smiling and thinking of the kisses when I turn back to Joe, to witness him, eyes closed, pulling the slimiest and stringiest bogey from his nose and swing the thing straight onto his tongue as if he were eating an oyster. I see the bobbing up and down of his Adam's apple as he swallows it. Joe eats his bogies. That tongue. It was in my mouth. I feel a wave of nausea as he opens his eyes, fresh from appreciating his recent snack. He registers my face. My eyes open wide. The frown. The heavy breathing. The struggling to keep my gag reflex under control, but I can't do it. I can't keep the nausea at bay. I feel the rush of my cheese salad baguette being evacuated from my guts, up my throat, and uncontrollably from my mouth. It sprays against Joe's face. His shoulder. His chest. His little trouser torpedo which has shown no sign of abating. His knees. Then somewhat ironically onto the floor and splashing up against his shoes. One spray. All I can taste is onion from the salad. My chin feels cold from the rapidly cooling sick that drips from it into my lap. Joe is speechless. Just sits. His dark brown eyes blink beneath the orange, and beige, and white, and green. His too-blue jeans turned darker from the liquid. His savage snow tiger contained in a cage of bile.

"I'm-" I try to say I'm sorry. But am I? *He* was the one who put his tongue in my mouth when *he eats his bogies.* He should be wearing a sign to warn people like me off. Still he says nothing.

"You," I croak, "you eat your bogies."

It's all I can do to not coat him in sick again so I rise from the bench. I use the sleeve of my cardigan to wipe away the sick from my mouth and chin, and I run. I shouldn't. I'm better than that. But I can't help myself. The sound of the world is drowned out as I stumble away from Joe. I leave him there. Silent. Dripping. Covered in my dinner. From our date. Our *pre-date date.* There won't be another. There can't be. Not after this.

***

He finds me outside the residential home. On a memorial bench for a woman named Barbara. I'm withdrawn. My hands clasped around one another and my knees pulled in. My face stained with tears. He was supposed to be a good one.

"It's just something I've done since I was a kid," he says, standing over me as I stare into the trees, "it's harmless."

I don't look up at him. Don't respond.

"It's just dirt," he continues, as if justifying it to me will make things any better, "don't you sniff up and swallow the snot anytime?"

"It's not the same Joe."

"It *is* the same. It's the same stuff."

He sits down beside me. My sick has dried on him. He hasn't even bothered to try to clean it off. He tries to rest his hand upon mine but I move it. He sighs.

"I like you Sara," he says. I thought I liked him too but. I can't even think it. "I thought we had a connection, you can't kill it for something like this. Hundreds of people eat their bogies. Thousands."

"Stop saying it, it's gross, and you *had your tongue in my mouth!*"

"Okay, I'm sorry about that, but I'm not going anywhere."

We each sit in silence. The breeze whistles through the trees around us. Surely I'm right to be grossed out by this. *Thousands* of people? Somehow I doubt it. I feel a twitch against my thigh, and look down to see his hand on the bench. His little finger attempting reconciliation. The white flag pinkie. I'm still upset. Angry. Furious even. I can't say anything.

"You buy *Granny Sluts* for your granddad. Some people might think that was pretty bad," Joe says. Doesn't look at me. He's just talking into the air. Yes Joe. Some people *might* think that was pretty bad. But I love my Granddad and if buying him a mucky magazine to enjoy in his own time is bad, then I'm bad. But I *do not eat my bloody bogies and kiss people with my horrible bogey tongue!*

"We could put it to a public vote. Like on telly. I'm sure you'd come off worse," I mutter. He laughs.
"I'm sure I would."
"You must be colour blind with your stupid mismatched clothes," I mutter. He laughs again.
"Anything else?"
"Scared of stupid stickers."
"You have an ejector seat for your feet," he counters.
"Can't talk to girls without throwing up."
It continues like this for a few minutes before I'm laughing too. We're sitting here tearing petty strips off each other and the shackles of disgust slowly but surely get chipped away, the coldness begins to thaw, and his white flag pinkie edges ever closer up my leg, until his hand comes to rest on my thigh. His face suddenly takes on an air of seriousness and he frowns.
"What?" I ask.
"I'll stop doing it, you know? I'll stop-"
"Don't say it," I interrupt. We've gotten round to being something close to friends again and I don't want him to ruin it.
"But I'll stop, I promise, I like you too much to spoil it with that," he smiles. Squeezes my thigh. I return his smile and again today I feel this warm fuzzy feeling. It's not been love at first sight, but this weird connection makes it something as close to it as I could ever hope to experience in real life. My hand slowly creeps to his and our fingers intertwine. Wrapped up in each other. I feel nice. This feels nice. I smile and watch a squirrel scamper across the grass. It stops to sniff at something, then my eyes follow it as it goes on its merry way into the bushes. This contentment stays with me as I turn to smile at Joe but he has his eyes closed. His little finger is burrowed deep in his ear. It twists and prods hard.

He pulls the finger from the orifice and opens his eyes. Oblivious to me. He scrutinises the deep brown sticky wax that sits on the tip. Then to my utter horror his tongue creeps from his mouth, and with the tip of his pink slug he takes a taste of it, before once again registering my horrified face, and then the second torrent of vomit that's rained down upon his face in a day.

THE TALE I SAID I'D TELL

I was asked something once. By a friend of mine. He asked how I got this scar on my cheek. This constant reminder of how fucked up my life was. I told him I'd tell him another day, but I haven't been in touch with him for a while, and I'm ready to tell the story, and you're all I've got to tell it to. No offence or owt. I'm not saying you're not good enough to hear it. But I'd prefer that you were somebody else, that's all.

I killed people. For money. That's what I used to do. For a job. I killed people. I didn't discriminate. If my paymaster pointed me in a direction, and was willing to pay the price then sure as hell I'd go in that direction, and I'd wipe out whatever I needed to. Whoever I needed to. Like I say, it was my job.

So, anyway, back in ninety nine. I was twenty. Still wet behind the ears in all aspects of my life. I was a late bloomer, you could say. Lost my virginity in Blackpool on my eighteenth birthday to a hooker named Mandy. My mates had had enough of my lies of encounters with girls they'd never meet because they didn't exist, and on my eighteenth birthday they paid for me to actually pop my cherry. They were good friends. This isn't part of the story really, it's just a bit of background information for you to understand how inexperienced I was in life. I was shy. I was nervous around women. Mandy made sure I had a good time though, said all the right things, made all the right noises. I thank her for that. Wherever she is.

After the shackles of virginity had been blasted away, I felt a confidence in myself that I'd never had before. I could look at the world through new eyes. You never really know what effect that virginity has on you until its cloud is lifted from your brain. I focused on other things in life. Like making money. Drug dealing. That was a thing around our end in the late nineties. It's probably still a thing really. But in my life it was *the* thing. I'd buy a block of solid hash on tic from a dealer called Dave and then hang around Wythernshawe selling shitty deals to the other teenagers. Usually fiver deals and tenner deals. It kept me in CDs and it kept me in beer. My mam never really asked for board. We were already fiddling the council as it was, I knew we were, and she knew I knew, so we all just did our own thing and used the house as somewhere to sleep. I spent most of my time round a bloke called Black Rob's, using it as a place to sell my shitty deals and a place to hang about. There was always somebody at Black Rob's who wanted a bit of smoke. We'd sit around, talking crap, sucking up on bongs, dropping bombs of speed, drinking beer, and then dropping the occasional jelly. All the while we'd be listening to tunes. Some of the lads liked happy hardcore, others were all over the trance shite, but my thing was proper old school sixties rock. My favourites were Creedence Clearwater Revival. I enjoyed nowt more than being monged off my tits and listening to dirty guitars. What can I say? It was our thing back then. We didn't have much else to do on our estate.

So, it was one of these nights at Black Rob's that really set me on my path to real life badness. None of that penny weight deal of hash shite. Real, actual badness.

We were all there. The usual bunch. Me, Black Rob, Lee Jones, Ryan Davies, and a kid we called Winnit. We called him that because he was always hanging off of our arses, everywhere we went there was always Winnit. I'd paid up with Dave and then got another nine bar on tic. A nine bar is nine ounces of solid hash, by the way. I always had enough to cover my own smoking needs on top of what I'd sell to make money, and that night I was feeling a bit generous so I was sharing out the spliffs and bongs with the rest of my pals. Most of us were just about passed out by the time it happened. There was a bang on the window. Lee and Ry barely stirred from their stoned states of mind, and Winnit was out cold. There was only me and Black Rob anything like compus mentus. I looked at Rob and he looked at me. Neither of us much bothered for going to investigate, but the bang came again, only this time it was three hard fisted smacks against the panes.
"Oi! Watch yerselves!" shouted Black Rob, "you'll smash me fookin' windows!"
The three hard bangs came again, so I stood up and went to pull the curtains open, ready for giving shit to whoever it was. Just as I opened the curtains there was this almighty crash. My world went black.

I woke up in the hozzie later that night. My mam looking down at me with tears in her red eyes. I dunno if they were red from crying or the booze, but it didn't really matter. She were there. She told me that whoever it were had lobbed a great brick through the window, straight into my face. A shard of glass sliced right through my cheek, they had to leave it in until they got me into the operating theatre, then I needed twenty odd stitches in my mush just to keep me from having two permanent mouths. They said I was lucky to still be able to see out of any of my eyes. That's what they said. They never said at that point whether they caught the cunts that did it or what. Never said owt about any of that. Just kept talking about how lucky I was to be able to see.

Now, while I was in hospital, I wondered some stuff. Like, how comes the coppers weren't there to question me about the nine bar I had in my possession. Or at least, I *thought* I had in my possession. I wondered when the arse was gonna fall out of my money making drug dealing schemes. They said nowt though. Little did I know the reason they never said owt about it, was the fact that there was no nine bar at the scene of the crime. They'd had away with it. Totally cleaned out Black Rob's place. Kicked the shit out of him, as well as the stoned and already unconscious bodies of Lee, Ry, and Winnit. Winnit was on life support, they said. Now, as sad as Winnit being on life support was, there was always this thing that kept going through my mind. *What is Dave gonna say?* I owed the cunt a fair few hundred quid. Not thousands, just a couple of hundred quid. But I didn't have the drugs to sell to make that money up. Dave was not a reasonable man. Dave was the kind of man to threaten his own granny if he thought she was holding out on him. Every time I grimaced at the thought the gaping wound in my face pulled against the stitches and cause me agony, but I couldn't help it. I'd cry both tears of agony as well as fear of whatever it was that Dave might have planned. The unknown. Eventually they filled me with morphine and I drifted off to a happy place.

They let me out a couple days later, and I was laid up at my mam's house. I suppose you could call it home, in as much as the council still gave mam money for me to be her official live-in *carer.* It was her turn to care for me though, and she undertook the task with disastrous aplomb. She stumbled around the place, hammered, spilled scalding hot soup all down my legs one day. Fell onto my face another, tearing open the wound once more. I screamed the house down and had to have my stitches reapplied. She was a shitty, useless mother, my mam. But she was my mam, what could I do?

One day, she was passed out, steaming drunk, and no amount of knocking from whoever it was outside would rouse her from her slumber. The knocking kept coming louder and louder, so eventually I got up. Dragged myself to the door. My heart sank as I saw the distorted figure behind the patterned glass. Dave. He was looking right at what would have been the distorted figure of me on the other side, and he gave this smile.

"Dave, alright?" I said to him, sheepishly.
"Rufus, my man, I heard you got yourself in a spot of bother," he said to me, this evil look in his eyes, "that looks nasty as fuck."
He was referring to my face wound. I nodded and gave a pained smile.
"Yeah, it's sore," I said.

His face softened.

"I heard you got your stuff nicked."

"Who told you that?"

"Is it true?"

"Well, yeah, but I can get your money," I said to him. Hoping that he'd give me some time.

"How you gonna do that then kid?"

I paused. I couldn't answer that. I had no idea how I was gonna make the money to pay him back.

"I dunno," I said woefully, "but I will, just gimme a week to get back on my feet."

"A week?" he said, "you ain't gettin' a week, kid."

I looked at him through pleading eyes, didn't say anything.

"I tell you what you can do to make it up to me," he said, I didn't want to know but he was gonna tell me anyway, "I've got a quick job for you. Won't take long. You might even make a profit out of it."

Now I was interested. Not only did he give a lifeline, but he was giving me a lifeline that left me in profit!

"Okay?" I asked, quietly, not wanting to appear too eager.

"You see, I know exactly who did that to your face. It weren't what you had what they were after. Rob was holding summat for me, and they've got it. I want it back. I want you to get it back for me."

"What have they got?" I asked.

"Something very important to me, kid," he said, "but if you get it, and you do it well, I might have a few more jobs lined up for you."

"What kinda jobs?" I asked.

"Ones that'll need this," he smiled, pushing a package into my hands. I looked down. It was a gun.

THE SHORT VERSION

So I'm gonna tell you a story, right? It's not about me, or anything that happened to me so don't expect any first person, inner monologue, here's-what-I-think-about-the-weather bullshit. No, it's sort of about how something you do can mess with everybody around you. You could say it was like a chaos theory story. The butterfly flapping its wings. Or you could say it was how one poisonous fuck destroyed the lives of everybody he came into contact with. Fucked up the lives of people he will never meet too. You could say it was probably more that than anything else but you're free to make you own mind up. You're a grown up, after all. It'll probably go this happens, that happened, he said, she says, punchline. I might even fuck with the tenses a little bit in the heat of the moment. Okay? Okay. I mean, what's the worst that can happen? You don't like the tale I have to tell and you go and tell your pals how you wasted half an hour listening to some piece of shit story by some arsehole that can't even get the ending right? No, that's fine by me, and even though you know I can't tell a story for shit, you'll stick it out, you'll sit there and listen. You want to see where this is going. Except you, Mr or Mrs *Post* Post Modern, yeah, you're gone right, about, now. Don't like the device. Shithead thinks he's clever. Nah, I'm just a dude with a tale to tell, and a wee bit of time to tell it. So you have a choice. You want the long version or the short one? You see what I did? I gave you a choice you can't even make, that's how annoying this piece of shit story's gonna be. It's a long story, but I have places to be, so don't get comfortable cause you're getting the short version.

Okay so let's start with Lee. Lee's a liar, amongst other things. When he was ten he killed a puppy. Stole it from a yard on his street, just snatched it right out of there. Carried the poor little bastard about a mile to some abandoned waste ground. Hand over its ginger snout. This is back before the councils and property developers snatched up any spare land and built identikit suburbs all over them. Yeah, Lee the liar took that puppy out of sight and earshot, and he beat the shit out of it. Lights in on fire. Laughed while he did it. He's gonna leave the poor little bastard to burn. Only, the thing is, Lee just can't leave things be. So he drags the flaming carcass and he tosses it into some dry grass. The dry grass flames up quick as hell. Lee stands there. Waits until it's out of fucking control, then skips on home, stinking of smoke. When he gets home his mum asks what he's been up to. Lee said he'd seen two local kids playing with matches, said he'd tried to stop em but they told him to fuck off. He says this to his mum, uses those words. *They just told me to fuck off.* Lee's ten remember. Ten year olds aren't supposed to know that kind of filthy language so his mum thinks he's quoting these two mystery kids verbatim. Pulls him close, holds his head against her bosom and tells him things will all be fine. That she'll protect him. The sneaky little fucker smiles, and all the while some poor girl five doors down is crying her fucking eyes out. Wanted to know where Freckles the spaniel could be. Now that little girl. Her name is Jenny. She loved that dog. This is back in the days before computers. Before mobile phones. Before Facebook and Twitter and all of that shit. This is when, if you wanted to call your pals or your family, you had to stand in the hallway, receiver to your ear, curly wire spiralling down to a cream, or green, or brown base which sat on a tall circular table by the front door. If you were lucky. If you weren't so lucky you had to take a pocketful of huge ten pence pieces to the red phone box three miles away and make that call. So Jenny, all she has at her disposal to be able to make a public plea for any kind of information is a bunch of lined paper that she'd ripped from her dad's notebooks, and a pack of felt tip pens. Young Jenny scrawls up some crude posters. Dog missing. Gimme my dog back. Have you seen Freckles? That kind of thing. Jenny takes these posters and sticks them up around the small mining village that she and her family live in. One of those kinds of places where everybody knows everybody. At least one of every family worked in the pits at any one time. Until the strikes. Until Thatcher. You know? Everybody knew everybody. So it's this knowledge that leaves Jenny's mum and dad feeling secure about their little girl wandering about on her own. They were called Karen and Steve. Her parents. That was their names. Jenny's just about put up her last poster when a car pulls up behind her. Some said it was a brown Volvo. Others a cream Opal Manta. Another witness said it was green. A green Ford Escort. Witnesses said that the man inside rolled down his window. Calls Jenny over. You could only assume that the guy has some sort of information about Freckles. The poor little bastard. Jenny skips over to the car. The car pulls away. No more Jenny. Like gone in a puff of smoke. Like magic.

Except it wasn't magic. They found her body four
weeks later, by a railway track. Mutilated. *Messed
with*. The guy that found her. In his nightmares he
saw her blue, bloated face. Staring up at him from the
long grass beside the tracks. She talked to him
though. In his nightmares. She talks to him and tries
to tell him who did it to her. Only, in his dreams she
goes all muffled the second she's about to reveal this
name to him. It kills him that she can't tell him. Only,
it's just his subconscious talking to him. There's no
way his dreams could tell him the name of the kiddy-
fiddling murderer. The guy that found her, his name
was George. George Chambers if you need to know
his full name. He worked for British Rail. This is back,
before they privatised the rail system. He was doing a
routine task, checking on a signal. Left his pal back in
the van, went up ahead on his own and never made it
to the signal box.

Oh, you should probably know that all of this.
With the way-back-when stuff. The year we're talking
about is nineteen eighty four. Early nineteen eighty
four. Not the Orwellian one. The actual real one.
Tommy Cooper died live on stage. The Miners' strike
kicked in. If you're more inclined to mark your years
in popular culture terms it was the year The Smiths
released their debut album. Just so you know.

So George Chambers. He can't sleep at night.
Not with the mental torture that he's subjected to.
The people who had it worst though, were her
parents. Karen and Steve. She blamed him, he blamed
her. Then the Miners' strike came. You have two
people are struggling to keep it together in the midst
of their grief. Then the strike on top of all of it. Steve's
out there fighting alongside his brothers, in a year

that will effectively destroy their lives, and the ripples of the storm will be felt for at least another two generations. Karen was at home. Nothing to do but think. Wait for a man that she's growing to hate to return from the picket line. Grieve for the daughter that was snatched from the streets and snatched from her life. One day, maybe August or September of that year, Karen takes her own life. Money was tight. The tension between she and her husband even tighter. She sat at the tiny kitchen table. Covered in the red and white checked plastic sheet. The dinner plates with recipes printed on each one piled up in the middle. She smoked an Embassy filter. And another. Then she left the house. Didn't lock the front door. She stumbled down the road in the dressing gown she'd been wearing constantly for weeks. Cut a left at the end of the terrace and made her way to the B road that separated the village from the next. She whispers something that not even *she* can make out, then steps in front of a bus full of picket scabs. She was straight away dead.

Now jump ahead ten years. Nineteen ninety four. What you should know about 1994, is that Fred and Rose West are big news. Dennis Potter dies a week after his wife. Pulp Fiction, for the popular culture fans, is released. And our friend Lee, the liar. Well, he's nineteen, but not for long.

On his twentieth birthday Lee goes for drinks with his pal, Kev. Kevin Barker. That was his full name. No middle name. He was never christened. This is back when smoking was still allowed in pubs. Inside almost everywhere. When smoking was still good for you. When only real men smoked. The thing about Lee is that he can't help but alienate people with his lies. Only Kev has remained from the ever dwindling circle of friends he once ran with. This is predominantly because Lee has money, fraudulently attained from various claims for ill health. Lee uses this money to buy ecstasy pills for their nights out. Lee is generous with these ecstasy pills, hence, Kev shall remain a friend to Lee. On Lee's twentieth birthday he shares out the pills as the lads enter Visage nightclub, and they each swallow two. About three hours later Lee was telling a girl named Susan that she was the most beautiful girl in the building, and at the same time Kev was convulsing in a toilet cubicle, trousers round his ankles. Kev has been drinking a lot of water to ensure he doesn't dehydrate, and as a result he has overhydrated himself. His liver and kidneys are positively swimming. His body has shut down. Several minutes of panic, smashed down cubicle doors, emergency calls, chest pumps, inflated lungs, deflated lungs, ambulance arrivals, and loaded gurneys later Kevin Barker is being carried from the men's toilets, oxygen mask over his face, by two paramedics. Sheila Taylor and Barry Hendry. Those were the names of the paramedics. Kev is comatose. As Lee stood with Susan she wondered out aloud if any of Kev's friends were around at all. Lee shrugged and told her he was wondering the same thing. Kevin Barker was pronounced dead before the ambulance doors had even closed. At the same time, about a mile across town, Neil Jones has been severely beaten up by a trio of thugs who had drunkenly made sexual advances toward Neil's pregnant fiancée Amy, whose honour Neil was defending. An ambulance has been called but the closest one was diverted to attend the altogether more selfish emergency of Kev. The next closest one will not arrive for seven minutes. In

this seven minutes Neil Jones will expire from his
injuries. He has suffered a *cerebral edema*, or brain
swelling, in layman's terms. Neil's attackers. Two
brothers by the names of Brian and Dan Scott, and
their cousin Jordan Stevens were apprehended two
days later, and eventually each received nine year
sentences for the crime of manslaughter. Jordan's
mum, Heather. She blamed her nephews for dragging
her beloved son into the attack. Refused to believe
that it was he that initiated the violence as the
brothers claimed in the courts. Jordan was due to
begin a History and English degree at Liverpool's
John Moore University in the Autumn of that year.
Was proclaimed a bright boy by all who knew him.
Heather and her sister, Wendy. They fell out. With all
of the will in the world Heather and Wendy aren't
going to talk to one another. Secrets. Secrets which
have been held between them for years begin to leak
out. The fact that Wendy shits herself when she's
drunk. Heather's propensity for stealing. The
time Wendy caught Heather with Uncle Terry's cock
in her mouth when she was thirteen. Uncle Terry
isn't a real uncle. Uncle Terry was their dad's best
mate in the sixties. These were things that both
women would much rather remained untold but with
no way to halt the feud without being the weaker
party. In the midst of all of the mudslinging Uncle
Terry is called to task by various of his drinking
buddies at the Miner's Welfare Club. He was outed as
a predatory paedophile by much of the village.
Accusations begin to pop up. Victims come forward.
Police are brought in. Evidence is collated. Gardens
are dug up. Bodies are found. Girls' bodies. Young
girls' bodies. The widowed Steve, who lost his
daughter and wife ten years earlier receives a knock
at his door. Steve, who has been treated for

depression for the last decade. Who has never recovered. The same Steve who carries a picture of his two girls everywhere he goes. Not that he goes anywhere very often. Not since then. Steve gets a knock at his door and two policemen stand before him. They are young. They probably weren't on the force when Jenny was cruelly snatched from this Earth. The officers are DCI Daniel Flaherty and DS Mark Benson. They ask if he has a cousin named Terry Clarke. If the predatory paedophile Terry Clarke from the next village is that same cousin. Steve confirms that yes, they are one and the same. Twos are placed alongside twos and fours are created. So the years went by. Arrests made. News broken. Stories told. Stories forgotten. Millennia seen in. Technology improved. Lies told.

2004. Another ten years have passed. Harold Shipman ends it all in his prison cell. Iraqi militants chop the head straight off of Ken Bigley's neck. For those of you who like to mark your years in popular culture events. Those of you who by now have spawned a few little versions of yourself, this was the year that Peppa Pig was first on the TV. Channel five. If you care. Another who'd spawned some offspring along the way was Lee. If you're aware of the notion of sarcasm you'll understand the tone when you're informed that Lee was a great dad.

So, Lee had six children. Those six children had five mothers between them. Those five mothers had three new boyfriends between them. Those three boyfriends had eight convictions for assault between them. These aren't numbers that bode well for the delightful fruits of Lee's loins. By the end of the year Lee will only have four children. One

Saturday morning in July. A summer morning. The rain is pouring down. Battering the front window of the council house that is rented by one of the aforementioned mothers. Kelly. Kelly Finnegan. Behind that front window sat the hopeful, but not expectant faces of Ashley and Callum. Twins. Now, Ashley and Callum had been unreliably informed by their mum that their Dad, our hero Lee, would be coming to collect them to take them swimming for the afternoon. In order to further excite the boys Kelly has also offered the possibility that a Happy Meal each may also be on the cards, if they behaved themselves. The boys waited from nine o'clock. The promised visit from their father was pencilled in for half past. Predictably that time approached and passed. As did ten o'clock. Then half past. The boys become anxious, and unsettled. Kelly's new boyfriend Tony, a bouncer in town, is still in bed after the night shift, and is not to be disturbed. The boys know how he gets. Kelly knows how he gets. Hushed and urgent warnings to keep it down go unheeded, and then a series of bleeps. Dadada, daaa daaa. Dadada. Dadada, daaa daaa. Dadada. Now, this is back when, unless you had money to burn, mobile phones could make calls, could send and receive text messages, and you could chase a little pixelated dot around your screen with an ever increasing line. They called that game *Snake.* This is before you could have the latest number one song as your ringtone. You got a high pitched little piece of Morse code instead of the latest hilarious comedy catchphrase. Kelly does not have money to burn, so Kelly's Nokia 5510 has a text. It's from Lee. Something came up. He's busy. He'll come next weekend. Maybe. If he can. The boys are distraught. Each makes the other worse with the ever increasing wailing. Kelly's warnings to be quiet became ever more desperate. They would wake Tony up. It's no use. Lee has let the boys down one too many times. They hate him. They don't want to see him anymore. Then *THUMP.* The ceiling shakes. *THUMP.* Tony's other foot strikes the ground. Still the boys wailed. Inconsolable. The noise starts to grate on every single one of Kelly's nerves. She gets annoyed. Then angry. She begins to screech for her children to be quiet, over the top of them refusing to be quiet. Tony appears at the bottom of the stairs in only his Calvin Classics boxer shorts. Three pounds for five pairs on the market. He's had four hours sleep. He was tired. He's angry. He only knows one way to shut this noise up. *SLAM!* Ashley. Out cold. *CRACK!* Callum's weak frame hits the wall. Only Kelly's banshee wail continues, until a heavy backhanded slap breaks her jaw. Knocks her unconscious. Silence. Tony sighs. Returns to bed. Sleeps. Is woken up three hours later by a shaking hand of a child. A hand fearful of further retribution. A hand belonging to Ashley. Wants to know why his mummy and brother won't wake up. Says his head hurts. With a little more sleep to his name Tony is moved to investigate. Finds the bodies. Panics. Ashley appears. Quivering lip. Face swelling beneath the purple blue bruise. Asks again why mummy's not waking up. Tony said nothing. The tiny hand that's pulling on his makes his skin crawl. This witness to his crime. The only witness. Tony wondered to himself how many other people knew he had been seeing Kelly. Not many, if any. Tony makes his decision. Walks out of the house by the back way, and leaves three corpses behind him. Three weeks. That's how long it took. Three weeks to notice any of the young family were missing. Lee didn't notice. It was the smell at first that alerted the neighbours. Mrs

Feeney. Three doors down. The closest neighbour on a rapidly diminishing estate. This is back when the councils started to clean up the shitty estates. Any time a family moved out or a heroin addict died they'd board up the doors and windows. Leave the place empty. Until the whole street was empty and they'd knock it down. Sweep away the remnants of a thousand lives gone by. Then the next street would go. Then the next. Then they'd build up a whole new estate. Bright orange suburbs with a park made of wood on the old green. But no, this is back in that *period of transition,* and Kelly had no next door neighbour. No next door but one neighbours. Just Mrs Feeney, three doors down. She didn't go out much herself. She had a carer by the name of Sally. Sally White. That was her full name. Sally Jane White, if you want to be pedantic about matters. Jane was her mum's mum. So Sally comes round on her twice weekly visit and the stench is something awful. She can't get more than ten feet from the house before she can taste it. Rotten meat. Blood. Shit. From where the bodies evacuated their bowels. The closer she gets to Mrs Feeney's house the more scared she is that she's gonna walk into an old dead body. Like maybe Mrs Feeney fell down the stairs. Cracked her skull open. Maggots taking their lunch straight from the brain. Only, she creeps into the house to find Mrs Feeney watching TV without a care in the world. The police get called. Bodies taken away. Poked. Prodded. Post mortems and what have you. Lee gets questioned. Where were you at the time? When did you last see? Can you think of anybody who might want to hurt them? Lee has alibis. Last saw them three months ago because Kelly was always busy. They were angels. Cries his crocodile tears. Goes about his life. Nothing more thought on the matter.

Tony, on the other hand. Poor Tony. He was torturing himself. Living with the guilt. Couldn't eat properly. Three weeks is a long time to eat barely anything. This hulking monster of a man slowly deflated. He stopped working. Didn't phone in or anything. Just stopped going. Then the TV started talking about the bodies of a young family. Kelly. Callum. Ashley. Found dead. Appeals for witnesses. Tony stays in hiding. Just watches TV. Looks for news. It's big news for a few days. Then a bus crash in Spain. Three Britons aboard. That's it. His crime forgotten. Or seemingly forgotten. As far as the law goes he's got away with it. But his guilt. You can't hide from what's in your own head. No chance. You can try but it always returns. Finds you. He's been drinking. Heavily. Now, Tony has never been a big drinker. His body was always a temple. Hours spent in the gym. Honing perfection. What for? To let it disappear to nothing. That's what he's done. His muscular stomach became a flabby belly. His solid rock pectorals now turned to soft, water-filled tits. One day Tony shits himself, but doesn't bother to clean it up. Sits in it and laughs. A drunken, if-I-didn't-laugh-I'd-cry type of laugh. He can't keep it up though. His laughter turns to heavy sobs turns to tears turns to dry retching turns to bile turns to stomach cramps turns to too many diazepam turns to whiskey turns to hiccups turns to confusion turns to blue fingernails turns to double vision turns to a text to his mum confessing everything turns to sleep. Long sleep. Tony woke up in a hospital bed. A policeman by the door. An arrest made. He should have injected the sleeping drug. He might have succeeded. But he didn't. He fucked it up. Within weeks a judge gave him three life sentences. Lee received tens of thousands in criminal compensation for his loss. Pissed it up the wall though, invested the lot in shares in MySpace. The idiot.

Time drips slowly. So slowly by. By 2008 Lee has forgotten he ever had six kids. Happy to accept he's only got the four. Fortunately for him, three of them refuse to see him, even if he *does* want to get in touch with them for some selfish bullshit lying cunt reason. By 2011 *none* of his kids acknowledge that they have a daddy. Thirty seven year old Lee continued to live the life of a young, free, and single man. Even though he is riddled with disease. Herpes, Chlamydia and one of the Hepatitises. Don't ask which one. Lee indiscriminately shoots his tainted muck into any willing recipient. Including one Emma Rogers on one drunken night. By the bins behind the Coach and Horses pub. It's a forgettable knee trembler but it passes the time. Offers yet another notch for each of their bedposts. A week after that Emma Rogers meets the man that she'll eventually marry.

So here we are. The present. Late 2013. The year that Alex Ferguson stepped down as the manager of Manchester United, to the collective sound of sighs of relief across the entire football world. The world grinds to a standstill to wait to find out exactly what Prince William and his lovely wife are gonna call their kid. Again, for those of you who love to mark their lives in popular culture terms it's the year that the Rolling Stones took money grabbing to whole new heights, and denied you the chance to see their Glastonbury set on TV, unless you wanted to wait for the DVD. Yeah, sure, no fucking chance, Mr Jagger.

Remember Emma Rogers from 2011? The one who met her future husband just shortly after a brief encounter with our hero, Lee, the liar? Sure you do. Well, she's no longer Emma Rogers. No, she's Emma Steele now. Nee Rogers. Or Emma Steele (Rogers) on her Facebook page. Married to the handsome James. A soldier. Love at first sight and all of that. Married at Gretna Green. You can see all of the beautiful pictures online if you want to. Well, Emma has forgotten all about Lee, and that filthy piece of action by the bins at the back of the Coach and Horses. He's been relegated to her mental recycle bin. Only, Emma forgot to click *empty* on that recycle bin, and Lee's about to rear his ugly fucking head in a big way. You see, Emma and James have been trying for a baby for the last few months. It's all they want, more than anything else. They only have eyes for each other, they want to spend the rest of their lives together, and a kiddy would be the cherry on the top of that lovely cake they called life. Eventually they decide to see a doctor. Somebody that can explain why the hell they're not being fruitful in their quest for a child. Not a good idea. You see, Emma contracted Chlamydia from Lee. It's rendered her infertile. Not only that she's unknowingly passed the dread lurg onto her new husband. No way there's a baby forthcoming for this pair. Emma now has to track Lee down. It's not hard. He's all over Facebook. Everybody knows Lee. The pair go to speak with Lee. Only, he doesn't care. He laughs when the tearful pair spill their guts over their hopes and dreams. Tell him that he's ruined everything. Lee says he's clean as a whistle. Never had a disease in all of his life. That they're just unlucky. Shows them the door. Only, this makes James mad. Furious even. Can't understand why Lee's so damn nonchalant about the whole thing.

A fight breaks out. From the thumps and thuds the neighbours are inclined to call the police. They don't like domestic violence. Only, when the police arrive, they're met by a bloody, and shaking figure. A figure whose face drips with crimson sticky liquid. Whose broken knuckles are coated in pieces of skull and brain, and vomit. Who falls to his knees and cries. He knows his life is through. It was through the second he took a hold of Lee's head and smashed it over and over and over against the marble mantelpiece. Until the skull split open. Until every tooth had smashed from his face. Until the hard whacks gave way to squelching sloppy splats. Even when Emma pulls at his shoulders. Tells him to stop but he can't. He stands and plants heavy boot after heavy boot down on Lee's neck. Crushes his throat. Smashes his spine. Turns what was once a standing, living, lying cunt of a person into a flaccid, torn, crushed mess. James was discharged dishonourably from the armed forces. Sent to Wakefield prison for the most violent of criminals. All he wanted was a kiddy. A baby with the love of his life. Lee took that from him. Lee paid for his actions, but still he continued to mess with lives after his death. Emma couldn't wait for James. No, wait, she *could* wait for him, but she. Shit. I've lost where I was. Okay. So James went to prison. Lee was buried. Fuck, I've totally fucked this up. There was supposed to be a moral. That's what's supposed to happen with stories. You're supposed to get a happy-ever-after. You're supposed to feel satisfied with the time you spent listening to the story. You're. You are. A fucking idiot. I told you I'd fuck it up. I told you I couldn't tell a story for shit. I told you I had places to be too, so you just get over it. See you around.

CALL ME DR FUCK KNUCKLES

John stared intently out of the window as the car rolled through the leafy suburb in Sheffield. Each house had at least two cars in their secure driveways. They weren't cheap cars either. Alternating between huge Beemers, Mercs, and the occasional Roller. It was nothing like the jam packed terraced streets that he was accustomed to. His own street where Helen would often have to park two roads away because you couldn't even squeeze a bus ticket between the rusted bumpers of the thirty year old bangers which lined the front of the garden-free houses. There were no kids here, either. No snotty nosed urchins left to their own devices for days at a time, screeching at one another from one end of the backings to the other, dodging bins and dog shit as they raced from the top to the bottom on brakeless bikes. From his vantage point he could see evidence of children around these houses though. Sandpits, basketball nets, bikes, footballs. A different class altogether. These kids doubtless had nannies, or au pairs. They were called babysitters where John came from. Or older brothers and sisters.

"Nervous?" asked Helen, her hand dropping down onto his thigh and squeezing it affectionately. He turned and smiled at his girlfriend non-comittally. Was he nervous? Just slightly. This was the first time he'd be meeting her parents. Of course he'd met girlfriends' parents in the past, and they were usually pain free affairs. It was always just a case of say the right things, laugh at the right places, and generally behave yourself. Don't drink too much, that was a standard rule. It would inevitably lead to spraffing shit in the dad's direction, staring at the mum's tits, and worst of all, in his own experience, sleepwalking and subsequently sleep-pissing on the dog. Once, that happened, and it never happened again.

The car rolled further along, slowing in front of huge black gates flanked by marble balls on top of limestone columns. Beyond the gate was a red brick driveway which stretched up towards the opulent three storey house, surrounded by evergreens, the tips of which reached almost as high as the house itself. They waited briefly before the gates, Helen honking the horn in a short sharp blast.

"You'll be fine," Helen said as the gates lurched into life, a low electronic hum audible as they crept slowly open, "just remember what I said about my dad, he can be a little strange, just humour him."

Helen parked the car beside a black Lexus, and turned to him, her blue eyes sparkling with a smile beneath her blonde fringe which had slipped just slightly out of place, "seriously, just take everything he says which a pinch of salt," she said, bringing a hand up to move the errant fringe strands, "he only does it to put you off. Please don't let him put you off."

"I'll not, it'll take more than being weird to put *me* off," grinned John, and it really would. Helen was by far and away the most attractive, and just genuinely *nice* woman he'd ever had the good fortune of meeting. She was generous to a fault, and had so far proved severely lacking in bad bones in her body. Or bad words said against her. Her eyes always seemed lively and excitable. Affectionate. They worked in tandem with her perfect mouth and the two pronounced dimples which creased into her cheeks whenever she beamed at him. He always held a doubting feeling that he was punching several notches above his weight, but her disarming smile and affable way never failed to put him at ease. If she didn't like him, then she simply would not be with him. He leaned over to kiss her tenderly on the lips, taking a deep sniff of her perfume. Boudoir, by Westwood. He didn't know he liked it until he smelled it on her, "come on gorgeous, let me at him."

"Helen, darling," purred Mrs James as she coasted down the front steps onto the driveway to meet the pair. She was an elegant woman, maybe in her mid-fifties, and looking very good for it. The money had obviously been spent keeping old age not so much at bay as locked deep into a chest in the attic that Harry Houdini would have trouble breaking out of, and unless he looked really closely, John reckoned it was money well spent. It was an excellent signifier of things to come, assuming he could keep a hold of Helen for that long.
"Hiya mum," said Helen, leaning in to hug, and kiss her mother on both cheeks, a theatrical double bill of *mwah* coming from the matriarch of the James household, "this is John."
John was accosted by a flurry of hugs, kisses and more *mwah* as Mrs James wrapped herself around him, cloaking him in the smell of her own perfume. It wasn't one he recognised, but it hung tight over him as she retreated to stand before them both.
"Hmm, he's a handsome one darling," she said, allowing her eyes to trail slowly from his top to his toe, and then back to his face. John said nothing, but

smiled with a false modesty, and turned to Helen who responded on his behalf.

"Isn't he just? My handsome rogue," Helen kissed him on the cheek and grabbed his hand, tugging gently, "come on, let's get inside, it's freezing."

John followed mum and daughter into the grand house. The hallway was wide, tall, and long, with hardwood flooring covered with a deep red, long carpet which ran the length. A stairway lurched up along the left hand side, and several doors to several rooms along the right hand side. Punctuated by paintings and photographs dotted along the walls.

"Beautiful house you've got Mrs James," said John, genuinely impressed with the place in the very short time he'd spent in it so far.

A family portrait caught his eye as they walked. On it Helen stood between her parents. Her dad stood proud alongside his girls. His wife, and their only child.

"Please, call me Cynthia, Mrs James makes me so awfully old. But thank you, Henry and I are awfully proud of it."

Cynthia. Not a name he would have fixed her with. She looked more like a Marion, or Felicity. The parents of any of his girlfriends always demanded first name terms, and John struggled with the familiarity. They'd only just met, but he would always force himself to apply the rule, however uneasy it felt. As they passed the first door he stifled the urge to whistle at the pristine cream leather corner suite which ran the lengths of two of the considerable walls inside the front room. It looked capable of housing at least fifteen arses, but in the kind of condition that said it saw one or two at any one time. Useful, but pointless in the same breath. Mrs James, Cynthia, swung a right at the next door, and spoke to somebody in that room. Presumably Henry. Mr James.

"Helen and her handsome beau are here darling, be nice, okay?"

John's attention anxiously flickered toward Helen who gave his hand a reassuring squeeze as they approached the doorway. Her smile beamed huge as a voice boomed from the room.

"Munchkin! My angel, good to see you!"

"Hi daddy," she said, pulling John with her into the chamber, before releasing her grip and approaching the man seated there. The room itself was smaller than the front one, but no less opulent. The man, Henry, Mr James, stood tall. Dark skin, weathered brown by countless trips abroad. To the villa in Marseille that Helen had told him all about, and shown him pictures of. It was a place he would very much like to see the insides of in real life. Maybe one day. If he could keep Helen for that long. She embraced her dad as she spoke, "did you enjoy the cruise?"

The pair parted and the older man nodded.

"Yes, yes we did. Aside from a pair of, ehm, *black gays,* in the next room. Most frightful. Put me off my dinner most days, right enough."

"*Daddy!* You know I don't like it when you talk like that!"

"Oh, hush, munchkin, I'm only joking. No, thankfully there were no blacks on the liner. Aside from the help, of course."

John caught himself suddenly aware of how shocked he must looked to the others, and became self-conscious, looking for somewhere to put his eyes without appearing to judge the man in his own home. Helen stepped back a touch and grabbed his hand, dragging him back into the room like a hypnotist. Her other hand slid down his arm affectionately as she made her introduction.

"Anyway, daddy, this is John. My boyfriend."

John released himself from her grip and lurched forward, one hand out in the direction of the apparent racist homophobe.

"Hi Mr James, ehm," he said, pausing a touch before adding a tentative, "Henry. Nice to meet you."

The older man grimaced, his upper lip and nose curling out of disgust, like he feared that John had fetched a fresh dog shit in on his shoe. Looked him up and down, much in the same directions as his wife had previously but with the polar opposite as far as appraisals went. This briefest of exchanges seemed to go unnoticed by the James women, and the man's expression switched quicker than as if it had been flicked at the switch. His face broke into a huge smile as he grabbed John's hand, squeezing firmly, and tight.

"John, good to meet you. But please, do not call me Henry, we are not well enough acquainted. You may call me Dr Fuck Knuckles."

There seemed not a glimmer of jest in his eyes as he spoke the sentence, his hand still gripping that of John's, ever tighter still. John had absolutely no idea of how to respond to that, and there was no way on Earth he was ever going to suppress the loud, and nervous laugh he then emitted. *Dr Fuck Knuckles?* Henry, Mr James, Dr *Fuck Knuckles* looked confused.

"Something you find amusing John?"

"Ehm. No," he responded, turning to see Helen shaking her head admonishingly, but with affection, at her dad. Was this all one big wind up? "No, nothing at all, Dr, ehm, Fuck Knuckles."

Dr Fuck Knuckles' face broke into a huge smile, the same blue eyes as Helen beaming at him from beneath the pitch black eyebrows which danced opposite one another like two rhythmic caterpillars. "Good!" he sang out, releasing John's crushed paw from his own, "I hope you kids are hungry. We've had Margot put a feast together!"

"So John," said Dr Fuck Knuckles as the pair of them sat together in the conservatory as Helen and her Mum pottered about the house somewhere talking about the cruise. The conservatory was attached to the rear end of the house. John had reflected that the entire downstairs of his own home could fit comfortably in this space, "what do you do?"
John shifted in his seat. Took a sip of his tea, letting out an involuntary *aaaaah* afterwards, which drew a disapproving look from the older man, but nothing was said.
"Well, I'm out of work just now, I was made redundant last-"
"Nonsense, you are never *made* redundant, if they have no use for you then you were *always* redundant," the man sniffed, "so what do you do if you are redundant?"
"I, ehm, I," John stuttered, not sure how to best venture forward in the conversation, but Dr Fuck Knuckles wasn't for helping him out, "I'm actually writing a book."
"A book eh? And what sort of a book are you writing?"
"It's kind of hard to explain-"
"Why of course it is. You're being very vague John, are you sure you're telling me the truth?"
"Yeah, I mean, Yes, Of course I am-"
"Are you going to cheat on my Helen as soon as you get the opportunity?"
"What? No! Really, Henry-"

"Dr Fuck Knuckles!"

"Dr Fuck Knuckles! I think the world of her."

"You're going to cheat on her the first chance you get aren't you? Don't try to kid a kidder young man, I can see it in your eyes you're a shady character!"

John could feel the anger rising into his chest and was doing all he could not to smack the old bastard right in his mouth, but Helen, she fought her way into his mind, calmed him. He sighed.

"Look, Dr Fuck Knuckles, I-"

"Helen, darling!" bellowed Dr Fuck Knuckles as the ladies joined them in the conservatory," John was just telling me about his book, how exciting."

Helen sat on the arm of the chair in which John was seated and began to play with his hair, oblivious to his flustered demeanour following the bizarre outburst by Hen- Dr Fuck Knuckles.

"Yes it is, it really is. I mean, he *is* still looking for a new job, but I think it's a really admirable way to spend your free time," she enthused, before kissing John on the head, "my boyfriend, the author."

John smiled, but couldn't say a word, as Dr Fuck Knuckles eyed him silently and venomously from beyond the sight of Helen.

An hour later and they were all around the table, John beside his girlfriend, his fingers intertwined with hers on his knee. Occasionally she'd tease him with wandering hands up to his manhood, but generally she allowed him the space to respond to her dad's increasingly erratic questions. Each time he brought something up Helen would give him a look, or shake her head, or exclaim *Daddy!* But for the most part she allowed the pantomime to run its course. The man was definitely out to push John's buttons but he held firm. He wouldn't let the old bastard kill his affection for Helen, nor behave in a way which would kill hers for him.

"Cynthia dear."

"Hmm?"

"Fetch the bubbly won't you?"

"Mmm."

Cynthia rose from her seat and elegantly retreated to the kitchen. John couldn't see why the hell a fine piece of woman like her would ever be attracted to the idiot head of the family, and reflected sadly on it as he watched her leave, until a sharp voice brought the room back tumbling to his attention.

"Did you just look at my wife's arse John?"

John coughed harshly, and turned to Dr Fuck Knuckles, and then Helen with fear and confusion in his eyes.

"No, I didn't! Helen I promise I didn't," he frantically pleaded, holding her hand tighter. Helen smiled at him and kissed him on the cheek before looking to her dad.

"Daddy, behave yourself."

"When that letch is undressing my wife, *your mother,* with his eyes, in *my* house?"

"In your house what dear?" asked the returning Cynthia, carrying what looked remarkably like two deep green plastic one litre bottles of white cider.

"Oh nothing, except I caught Helen's boyfriend sexing you with his eyes. *Sexing you!"*

"He wasn't sexing me were you John?" she purred, but her eyes sparkling with something that said *sexing* was exactly what she wanted from him. John coughed again.

"No, I wasn't, I really wasn't."

"See, dear? John says he wasn't. Shall I pour the bubbly?"

Dr Fuck Knuckles gave a short *hurruff* but allowed the situation to pass without further heckling, before standing to take the bottles from his wife. They *were* bottles of cider. Much the same as the kids around John's village would pour down their necks at an alarming rate, before stumbling around the place causing aggro for all and sundry. *And these people called it bubbly.*

"We got this in especially when we knew you were coming John. It's what you people drink isn't it?" Dr Fuck Knuckles said as he peered over to his guest.

"Ehm, sorry, me people?"

"Yes, council estate people, is this not the correct brand?"

The old bastard held the bottle closer to John for him to read the label, the brand was *White Power,* which perturbed John in several ways.

"Ehm, I don't really, I don't really drink cider. Especially not white cider. I'm more of a lager man."

"But I thought this was what you washed your heroin down with after you've been shooting up?"

"Daddy!" Helen gasped.

"Am I right? If I'm wrong then please tell me, I thought I was being a most accommodating host. I even purchased several wraps of it for you to inject later, I thought I might partake with you."

"I'm not a smack head, sir, Dr Fuck Knuckles," John said quietly, the man was wearing him out. Dr Fuck Knuckles opened the bottle of cider, and strutted round the table saying nothing as he poured the acidic and bitter drink into everybody's glasses. John felt Helen's hand again grab his, and rub the back of it with her thumb, offering a silent support for his experience. With his eyes he pleaded with her to take him away from that god awful man. He so wanted this to have gone well, wanted them to accept him, but Dr

Fucking Fuck Knuckles was making a very good show of showing him just how unwelcome he was. The old bastard sat back down, before raising his champagne flute filled with *White Power.*

"To Helen and John," he said without waiting for anybody else, before downing the drink in one. His face twisted out of all recognition. His eyes squeezed tightly shut, his mouth spazzing out, as the flavour of the cider hit his every taste bud. John stifled a laugh at the old bastard's discomfort. He was still Helen's dad, and no amount of will in the world was going to make him spoil her perception of him. He needed to do *something* though. He was being hung out to dry.

"Bloody hell, is that what you people really drink? It's like bloody battery acid!" he bellowed, tears streaming down his mahogany face. He grabbed a glass of water to attempt to wash away the remnants of the peasant juice.

John shook his head with a smile.

"I agree, Dr Fuck Knuckles, it's awful. I don't know why my people do it to themselves."

The meal passed, various cutting remarks were batted back confidently by John. He liked to think that he now had some sort of measure of what Dr Fuck Knuckles was all about. He said things to shock and provoke.

"Are you racist, John?"

"No, no I'm not."

"Ohh, I am. I really am. Brown people scare me."

"I suppose that's because you're from a different era, Dr Fuck Knuckles, when foreigners were the devil. Nowadays it's highly frowned upon to hold that sort of opinion, but I suppose you *are* in your own home, and a lovely home it is."

"Oh, well, what about bummers?"

"Bummers?"

"Queers, arse bandits, faggots?"

"Again, I'm perfectly fine with anybody's sexuality."

"Have you ever had a gay experience John? Have you ever let another man drive his chubby knob up into your-"

"Daddy! Enough!"

"Let him answer the question, darling, I'd like to know if my potential future son in law has ever let another man enter his back garden."

"No, I haven't, but thank you for considering me your potential son in law. That means a lot," said John, throwing an adoring look to Helen.

Dr Fuck Knuckles sat back, subdued. John had held his own so far, after a very shaky start. Perhaps this was what he wanted. For a suitor of his daughter to stand up to him.

"This food is delicious Cynthia, it really is, pass my compliments to the chef, please."

Cynthia eyed him, delighted, and licked her lips. She was a lovely woman. If John weren't with Helen he might really have made a play for her, Dr Fuck Knuckles or not.

"I will, my handsome guest, I really will. Helen darling, he really *is* a catch."

"I know, I think the world of him, and he does of me," she smiled, dropping her head onto his shoulder, "I've found a good one."

"Could I borrow him one time? I'd love to see what's under his clothes?"

John spluttered on his water at the last remark, attracting various titters from the others. Dr Fuck Knuckles included. He put his drink down and looked to Helen, gauging what sort of reaction she was going to give. There was no way she would go for it. No way at all. She must know that her mum was making a big joke, just something to flatter him.

"Yes, of course you can," she said, without even a hint of humour, "is that okay with you John?"

"What?" he asked, his mind completely and utterly blown.

"Cynthia, tell John about our sex parties," Dr Fuck Knuckles intervened, "tell him how many cocks you went through last time."

John didn't know what to do, or where to look. Helen look at him expectantly for a response to the invitation to fuck her mum. Cynthia wanted the same thing. Dr Fuck Knuckles, well he was getting tipsy, and looked to his wife to divulge the cock count from the last sex party.

"Well, John, can I take a look at what you're packing?" asked Cynthia, eventually.

"Go on, show mum your cock darling. She loves cock."

"Cynthia, didn't you get two in at once?"

"John, I've seen you looking at my tits all night, come and get them in your mouth."

"Suck mum's tits, darling. She loves getting her tits sucked."

"Cynthia, remember when Clive put it in your arse by accident?"

"If it's big, I'm really quite accommodating, John."

"Go on, see if mum can take your big cock, darling."

"Cynthia, remember when-"

"ENOUGH!" John slammed his hands onto the table, silencing the James family, he said nothing for a short while, calming himself down as best he could, before he spoke, "Cynthia, you're a beautiful woman, and in another life, I'd do all of those things to you, and more. Dr Fuck Knuckles, you are a mental case. An absolute *fucking* crackpot, but I've put up with your racist, homophobic shit for Helen," he said,

addressing the parents, before turning to his girlfriend, "and *Helen,* do I even know you?! What's with all the *fuck my mum* talk? Is that what you really want? Is that what I need to do to keep you?"
Her lips trembled. Her eyes glassed over. She said nothing, nodded, just ever so slightly, but she nodded all the same. He looked at her with sadness. She was beautiful. She was an absolute angel. She was as fucked up as the rest of them. But she was minted. John sighed, and unbuttoned his trousers.
"Fuck it, come on Cynthia, let's see what you can do with this."

THA DUNT COME FRUMT TARN
THA GETS NOWT FRUMT TARN

I'm bored. Bored of my every need being pandered to by hangers-on, and sycophants. Yes men. I'm not *always* right, but you couldn't tell. Sometimes I entertain myself by declaring something that both I, and they, know to be entirely false to be gospel true, and watching the slack-jawed confusion in their faces. Their eyebrows furrowing, the inner turmoil of their brains telling them, *that's wrong,* but their features twist and gurn, and their mouths betray them on my behalf, *that's exactly right Fintan.* This is my life. I don't work, my father did enough of that for the rest of us. He spilled an ocean's worth of blood, sweat and tears to make life easy for mother and me. *What a guy.* He was worth over six billion pounds when he died. Now I'm worth over six billion pounds. It was his intention to pass the business over to myself. It was my intention to sell it, so that's what happened. He'll be turning in his overpriced and luxurious cavern of a grave, next door to mother, still wrapped in her gaudy fur coat, diamond encrusted stiletto shoes, and that *fucking* pearl necklace. They died last year, together on private jet. The pilot got it into a little bit of trouble and nosefucked a massive hole into the moors. It was big news, you probably read about it. The dildo industry mourned one of its true pioneers, and his glamourous wife who got fucked seven ways from Sunday for the onanistic pleasure of anybody with an internet connection, she was also mourned of course, but for slightly different reasons. They left me as an extremely wealthy, and jaded orphan. Their methods of parenting were unorthodox to say the least. They exposed me to everything they did in their work from an early age. It wasn't in any perverted way, at least I don't *think*. My father worked on new and improved ways to massage a G spot from the comfort of our living room. Count Duckula bickering with his nanny, and Dangermouse solving badly animated mysteries would forever be tainted by the underlying soundtrack of a steady hum of a twitching latex cock spazzing out in his hands. Mother would be upstairs with her friends, a clicking super 8 film rolling round and capturing the heavy slapping thrusts of whoever was nailing her at that moment, Jacob the regular soundman hanging over them, ready to gulp into his recording device her theatrical wails of pleasure. Count Duckula's nanny would cry *I'll get it!* As whoever from above would yell *You're fucking getting it!* As I said, an orthodox childhood it was most definitely *not*.

***

I don't have many friends, if indeed I have any real ones at all. I'm surrounded by the aforementioned sycophants, but there *is* Danny. Danny amuses me, and has a very useful way of speaking his mind. He showed up at the house one day, asking if this was where the legendary porno slash musical *Annie, Take My Cum!* Was shot. Of course, mother was over the moon to have made such an impression on the boy, and invited him in to take afternoon tea. That was three years ago, and he never left. He was treated as a surrogate son of my parents, surrogate brother to me. He didn't see a penny of the inheritance, of course he didn't, but I allowed him to continue living at the house with me. I sometimes pay him to hurt himself, for example one time I sat in my dressing gown, one foot raised into the air, and paid him a thousand pounds to run face first into my heel. It broke his nose. I think he would actually do it for free but I have to do *something* with this money. As I said, he amuses me.

Aside from Danny there are the many members of the paid help team. I know they're stealing from me. But I don't care. I don't know how much they'd have to steal from me for it to make a difference to the six billion. The interest on that sum would swallow up any losses I make on thieving staff. I overheard the young scruffy lad, I don't know his name, to my face he's another of the *yes men,* but behind my back, he thinks I'm a cunt. He said as much himself. Fair enough, he's entitled to his opinion. The jewellery that he helps himself to, he calls that *Cunt Tax.* Yes, you heard correctly, Cunt Tax. Fair enough.

So I'm sitting in the lounge with Danny. What you need to know about Danny is that he's twenty nine, one year younger than my thirty, and he's originally from Sheffield, in the north. His hair is a mass of naturally curly dark brown locks. He has a perennial five o'clock shadow that he either maintains at such a length, or I just don't see him when he's freshly shaven. His wardrobe consists of dark grey jogging pants and green hooded tops. He claims that fashion, and brands are not interests of his. Comfort is his thing, he says. Fair enough. His blue eyes sparkle with mischief, and his fat nose seems to take a good percentage of his head, as far as coverage goes. He claims to have had his fair share of sexual encounters with a variety of ladies, but I'm dubious about that. He's not *bad* looking, but I don't know. His nose might put some people off.

"Finn," he says to me, he knows I hate it when he shortens my name, but he does it anyway, "if yer bored you should stop sitting around with yer finger up yer arse and get out, do summat with your life. Get a hobby maybe?"

A hobby. My hobby is hurting him for money, but I don't say that. I don't say anything.

"Reyt, what about you do a secret millionaire?" he's continued, seeing the indifferent look on my face, no doubt.

"What's that?" I ask, vaguely intrigued, but not enough to take his suggestion too seriously, but it's conversation.

"What? You never hearda Secret Millionaire?"

He sits forward, and all I'm thinking is that I hate questions like that, like, surely just asking *what's that?* Should be enough for him to understand that I've never heard of the concept. I don't say that, I just shake my head, *no.*

"Aww, it's crackin'," he says, "they send a millionaire to live in down an' out areas, y'know? Places where they're all unemployed or on smack or some shit, an' they take a cameraman with 'em and say they're doin' a documentary about some shit different, tell 'em all he's lookin' for work or some shit, an' he makes mates with folk, falls in love with 'em all and gives 'em money to make himself feel better about his own life, y'know?" I don't know. What I *do* know that it sounds positively horrendous. He sees this etched plainly across my face and goes on.

"No, no, honestly, hear me out, it's better than it sounds, it's actually good viewin'," he seems almost hurt by my physical indifference, and shifts in his

seat, "anyway, I'm not saying that you should go out and gi' all yer cash to scratbags, I'm sayin' you should go out and *pretend* to be one of 'em."
Interesting, I think.
"Interesting," I say. I still don't know enough of what he's talking about to venture further into this, but in my head I'm living it up like Rockefeller on a council estate, using people as doormats. I already like the idea.
"Yeah, what I'm sayin' is, people are wise to it now. It used to be that they'd be actually surprised when the fella reveals himself as a millionaire, but nowadays, they almost *know* he's gonna rip off the tracksuit and tell 'em he's minted. What I'm puttin' to yer, is that we go to some council estate, camera'd up to the eyeballs, start telling folk that you're some down an' out, lookin' for a job. You make pretend mates with some old dear, an unemployed spaz, and some charity case-" he stops, aware that I'm frowning, his palms facing me, telling me to hold my horses, "I said *pretend* mates."

***

I'm in my bedroom, poring over Bret Easton Ellis' *American Psycho* for what could be the hundredth time. Every time I read it I find a different possible outcome. Is it all in his head? Is some of it in his head and some of it real? Is it all real? I don't know. But it blows my mind, and it stretches the limits of my imagination. But still there's this niggling doubt, scratching at the floor of the back of my brain like a hamster trying to dig out of its solid plastic home, this overriding feeling that I'm just *bored*. As if on cue there's a knock at the door. Danny.
"Knock knock," he says.

"You don't need to *say* knock knock Daniel. You just knocked," I speak as I peer over the edge of my hardback first edition, "besides, you just came in, I don't think there was even a need to actually knock."

"Ah shurrup, I was wondering if you'd changed your mind about the Secret Millionaire thing."

This is what I like about Danny, he doesn't seem to even understand that I'm loaded, it means nothing to him. I feel like reminding him.

"I'll consider it if you punch yourself in the face," I say, Danny smiles and shakes his head.

"Easy stuff, you got nowt better than that? You must be feeling really down," he says with a sigh. He's right. I was just discussing my imagination getting a work out and then I go and spoil it all by suggesting something stupid like a self-punch to the face.

"Okay, fair enough. I'll consider it if you throw yourself out of my bedroom window. I'll give you ten grand too," I say, take that Daniel you Northern Monkey. He rubs his chin thoughtfully. My room is only on the first floor, if he lands correctly he'll be fine. If I'm lucky he'll break his legs and we can say no more about this stupid Secret Millionaire idea.

Danny goes to the window and peers over the ledge. I know without looking that his landing surface would be gravel. Tiny sharp pebbles just aching to take his fall. The silver lining is that they're quite deep too, so he'd be well cushioned. He looks at me doubtfully.

"Long way down. Can I take you up on that punch to the face?" he says into the air outside.

"No dice. You can leave through the door or the window but only one will be worth your while."

He's made his bed, he can bloody well lie in it. Preferably with a broken leg. Danny shakes his head again, he's going to bottle out. He disappoints me. I turn my attention back to *American Psycho*. I like to ensure that I utilise as few brain cells on indulging Danny as possible, they can definitely be better used elsewhere. Patrick Bateman is informing somebody that he's in *Murders and Executions* when the page flaps gently with a sudden breeze as Danny silently runs by me, by my bed, and out of my window. Five minutes later my door swings open once more.

"So are you going to think about it then Finn?" he says as he limps back into the room, a crimson red stain growing into the dark grey soft material of his jogging pants from where it looks like he's cut his knee, and badly too. He holds a hand under his armpit, if I had to hazard a guess I'd say he landed on his knees and used his hand to cushion his landing. Fair enough. I reach into the bedside cabinet and pull some wads of cash out, throwing them to the floor beside his feet.

"Did you break anything?" I ask, not a hint of concern in my voice. Whilst he crouches to collect the cash he shakes his head, no.

"I don't think so, it's actually not that far when you get out there, just got to judge the landing," he croaks through sharp intakes of breath as he puts pressure on his bad leg. I shrug, and raise my eyebrows.

"Want to go again?" Again he shakes his head.

"Nope, a deal's a deal, are we gonna go pretend to be secret millionaires or what?"

***

I'm only going along with this because it's something to do. Usually I spend my days wandering the corridors of the huge house. In my underpants. The hired help follow me round, clearing up messes I make. Occasionally I leave turds curled out on the side of the swimming pool, I let them see me do it too, and then I watch as they hurriedly clean it up behind me, refusing to reprimand me for my behaviour. I'm basically a very wealthy dog. Or a cat that isn't litter trained maybe, they're more disinterested. Cats, they're basically something that make people who like to talk to themselves feel more comfortable about doing so. That's what I am, I prowl around the place as if I own it, mainly because I do actually own it, and shit indiscriminately for my own entertainment. I don't watch television as it's something that's designed to make us stupider. Yes, stupider *is* a word. I refuse to plug my attention in to ridiculous people saying ridiculous things for the purposes of keeping idiots like you entertained. Idiots like Danny.. Animals do *not* do the funniest things. Britain does *not* have talent. I've never seen any of this dross, Danny keeps me well abreast of what you watch.

This is how we find ourselves where we do, thundering up the motorway to a town called Barnsley. Me in the back of the Bentley, Danny up front driving, his hand tapping on the steering wheel along to old Johnny Cash songs, him attempting to drop his voice down deep like Mr Cash. He's quite good at it too, but I'll never tell him that. The junctions tick gradually upwards, and by thirty four we're passing a huge green domed shopping centre, Danny tells me this place is called Meadowhall. He seems to think that it was originally going to be a prison, before it was sold as a shopping centre. He tells me that they have a basement entirely full of body bags in case there's a terrorist attack. He says that the locals call it Meadow*hell.* I can imagine. He says that as a child he would come here to hang out in the amusement arcade whilst his dad would play the gambling machine. *Hang out.* So crass. And I can't think of anything worse than rubbing shoulders with sticky faced loud wailing children, filling up on sugar whilst the weekend-father fritters away the remainder of the Christmas fund, in the hope of a slight rub of the green to save from him letting his family down for yet another year. At least the family that still won't accept that the longer he remains in their lives the further down he'll drag them all. Junctions thirty five and thirty six pass us by a Danny's still talking. He tells me that he used to see a girl from Barnsley.

"It was going so well, I thought she were a reyt nice lass," he says over the top of Johnny Cash telling us that he shot a man in Reno for the purposes of watching him die, "but I found out off one of me mates that she went home with five of 'em, and spent all night working her way through 'em, and not necessarily one at a time." His eyebrows rise, as if to ask me what I think of that.

"Sounds like a delightful girl," I say.

***

The plan, if you could possibly even begin to describe it as such, is simple. We've booked into the hotel which Danny describes as the most illustrious in the area. I would loathe seeing any of the others if *this* is the most illustrious. As far as I can tell its claim to exclusivity is the fact that it backs on to a golf course. *Swish*! From our HQ at the hotel we will venture out into the local communities, and Danny will claim to be a recently single man currently looking for jobs in a new area. This was my only condition. I would utterly *loathe* to speak face to face to the oiks that we are likely to encounter. He knows these people, this is where he comes from. We can go about this minor adventure for Danny's benefit, but I would play the role of cameraman. Even then I'm slightly wary of the role, since my only experience of cameramen in the past has come from the series of mullets and moustaches that would fill the large kitchen at our house, all taking a break from immortalising the hairy arse as it thrusts yet another erect cock into my mother. All the while our cook, Mrs Dodd, would be plating up eggs and bacon for their hungry bellies, and my father would be wandering around the house declaring that the *real-feel jelly* that he'd come up with for his new Power Suction Vagina just didn't feel real enough. He said it didn't have the correct viscosity. This was my childhood. So I am the cameraman in our little charade, Danny is our pretend secret millionaire, and the hundreds of natives we are to encounter are the stars. Danny tells me that people will fall for it. He says that they have seen this television show so much that when he arrives in their estate, the first thoughts running through the tiny minds of each of them is that he is the secret millionaire and they should treat him like a king, all the while waiting for him to drop the pretence and hand over a huge cheque for however many thousand pounds. Danny claims that this will *definitely* happen. Then when comes the time that he's about to reveal his true identity, that's when we disappear, laughing all the way back to Hertfordshire. I have to admit that, the natives aside, it does sound like rather an amusing ruse, something to do, you could say. It would certainly beat shitting on the side of my own swimming pool. At least for a week or so. I imagine I'll be bored by then.

***

The van pulls up into the grounds of the hotel, and Danny jumps from the driver seat, skips around the front and to the side door. He slides it open to reveal our technical kits, and pulls out a camera.

"Panasonic, professional imagery, they use it on actual telly shows, it'll really set you off nice," he explains. I don't know how or when he got this stuff. I don't ask, "it's really easy to use."

He tries to put the camera onto my shoulder, but I flinch and move away from him. He knows I don't like to be touched. I hold out my hands as if to request it that way. He complies and I find myself awkwardly holding it with my two hands. It's heavier than it looks. He fidgets near me as if he is itching to touch it again, but it's in my hands now, and I'm rolling it around, scanning it quietly for an *on* switch. It eludes me.

"It's just there," Danny points at a cluster of about fifteen buttons. I suppose he at least narrowed the target area for me. He's dancing in front of me, still itching to do the job instead.

"Do you want to do it?" I ask, holding it back to him, I would have preferred to find it myself, but the satisfaction pay-off is far outweighed by my irritation at his performance, I'd much rather he stopped dancing than find the damn thing myself.

Danny switches the thing on and hoists it onto his shoulder. A red light clicks on the front of it. I know from experience that this means he is recording.

"So Finn! Tell me a bit about yourself," he's saying, his fingers twiddling at the top, and from experience I know that when the lens dilates and constricts slightly that he's zooming in and out. A standard response from somebody playing with a camera. I used to be allowed a go on the film cameras as a child. Only between shooting would I be permitted to enter the room. The stench of a million flavoured condoms combined with the bleachy smell of sperm, made only more pungent by the heating unit, keeping our delightful cast members, my mother included, nice and warm whilst they wander around the room naked, stepping over wires and monitors to gain access to a scant refreshment table. With my flashback completed I return my attention to the black machine on Danny's shoulders, continuing to steal my soul.

"Fuck off Danny," I say, my hand reaching up to block the lens, my face turning away. I won't allow him to steal my soul.

"Stop being a poof," he says, almost hurt by my failure to play the game. The camera hangs heavy by his side, the lens raised slightly to face me. He must think I'm stupid.

"Stop it recording," I say, calmly and quietly, and he resigns himself to the fact that I will *not* play the game. I take the camera from him, and place it back into the van, already I'm starting to wish we'd not left the house, it's irritating the hell out of me, "I'll figure it out, just bloody drive us to this thing. Let's get it over with."

***

Danny drives us through this town. Various rabbit warrens and hovels pass us by. He says that he knows where we're going, but doesn't say much about it. He calls the place *Wuzzbra,* which sounds almost Australian, almost aboriginal. Wuzzbra. He says Wuzzbra has a Dale, a Village, a Common, and a Bridge. He says we're going to Wuzzbra Common. He says we probably should have thought about hiring some security to do this, but we're already in the moment now. If we get bored by the end of the day we can always go home. If it turns out to be utterly awful I might not even let Danny come back with me. We'll see how he behaves. I probably will.

We turn a corner and start our ascension of a winding road up a hill. The houses are small, and sit side by side in terraced rabbit warrens, each tributary drops down and evolves into a tight cul-de-sac. Each road has the tell-tale *dead* end sign. You know the one. The letter T. *Dead End*. It says so much. A single shoe hangs from the telephone wire above us, pulling the wire down and up as it is carried in the wind. The further up the hill we go the more barren and desperate the place becomes, which is in stark contrast to the vast green valley that opens up atop the hill of this place, Wuzzbra Common. The skeleton of a building that perhaps used to house some local shops, barely stands, and by it there's a bus stop which looks like it used to have glass in it. Every square inch of it has been raped by poverty and lawlessness. Gaudy spray painted words sit over faded spray painted words sit over marker penned outlines of times gone by. Even from our vantage point in the white van you can see it as a testament to each generation becoming gradually worse than the last. It's at this point that I'm suddenly less sure about our game, but Danny is already pulling up alongside a church, and it's gone a little far now. I'll put up with it for today but by evening time I expect we'll be on our way right back down the motorway, Danny up front and me in the back of the Bentley. He turns to me.

"Ready?" he says, smiling that stupid smile.

"Suppose," I say, shrugging, hoping that he senses my unease, but he's less aware of his surroundings than he is of himself, so I find myself staring at the empty space that he used to fill before he climbed out of the van and sauntered round to that side door again. I'm already sick of that grinding noise.

"You getting out?" he asks, calling over my shoulder from the doorway. I sigh, and unclick my seat belt, before I slide myself down from the seat and step onto the street. The crunch of smashed glass beneath my shoes goes through me, making my thighs tickle. It'll be ruining my soles. They cost me a fortune that I barely noticed had disappeared from my account.

Danny hands me the camera, already switched on.

"Okay, so we're clear yeah? Let me just wander about and talk to folk, you follow me with the camera," Danny instructs, and I'm about to respond in some way but I'm interrupted by a squeaking voice, which I turn to see belongs to a child of no more than eleven or twelve.

"Tha doin' mister?"

He could be years older, or younger than that but I've found that the longer in life I go the less skilled I am in estimating ages. The kid is adorned from head to toe in a matching black and white tracksuit. A cap sits atop his tiny pea head, not pulled right down, more balanced precariously on top. His hands explore the space at the front of his tracksuit trousers, I don't want to speculate on what else he's up to down there, but it's unbecoming. I don't say anything, and look to Danny to speak, but his attention is focussed elsewhere.

***

Before we know it we're surrounded by at least eight feral matching tracksuits. This is definitely an unfortunate turn up for the books. I'm looking to Danny to get us out of this because he's from this God awful county, he can talk to these people in an accent they'll understand. He's not saying anything though, he just keeps stepping back toward me with every step that the children take toward him. For a man who'll hurt himself for my entertainment he seems remarkably scared of being hurt here.

"S'camera fo'?" one of them says, I'm not sure it's a question. It just seems like a series of noises.

"I don't know what you're saying," I cannot resist the urge to say, and my face goes to battle with my emotions. At the forefront my face is desperate to show this *oik* how disgusted I am at him. It wants to convey confusion at the awful noises that his mouth spewed our way. But my brain is saying *no, be careful, you don't know what diseases these urchins could pass on!* The child looks perturbed.

"Thy on abaaart thee?" he says. I feel like I'm in a foreign country.

"Sorry?" I say, the confusion storms through my brain's barriers and displays itself in full glory across my nonplussed face. I look to Danny out of sheer desperation. I simply *cannot* understand a word these miniature scumbags are saying. He makes a play to get across to them, palms toward them in a gesture of surrender.

"Alright lads, we're meckin' a telly programme, about-" he starts, but another of the boys steps in and spits the darkest greenest glob of snot right at his feet. Beneath his cap his face appears to be twisting under in a greasy red, blotchy coating, like his spotty visage has been dipped in some magical polka dot candle wax. I'm struggling to keep my breakfast down.

"A thy a *Dee-Dah?*" He emphasises the noise at the end, directing it to Danny, but it's still just noise. I'm half expecting him to start emitting a series of clicks to communicate with his surrounded associates. Danny laughs, and it's nothing like as derisive as it would have been if I'd done it.

"I am aye," he says, I don't know how he can understand the urchin, "Blades born and bred me." He declares proudly. The kid smiles, and as he looks to the boy to his left his smile disappears and a twists into something altogether more savage.

"Fuckin' hate dee-dahs. Specially dee-dahs that knock abart wi' suvvern wankers. Telly camera cunts." Now I think I got *that.* I'm not having this, do they have any clue who they're talking to?

"Now listen, you little *oik!* Do you have any clue who you're talking to?" I step to them, only slightly, but immediately they bristle together, tensing up in the face of confrontation. The greasy faced leader spits at my feet, and his mucus not so much slaps the pavement as it does thunderclaps against it, such is the force he throws it out at, and the weight of his teenage snot.

"Fuckin' suvvern wanker wi' a dee-dah mate. A thar two bummers?"

"No, course not, I told you, we're shooting a telly programme
about-" Danny is interrupted once again. This is not my comfort zone. This is so far out of my comfort zone that my comfort zone is in another *time zone.*

"Shut yer fuckin' marf dee-dah cunt! Tha dunt come frumt tarn tha gets nowt frumt tarn!"

I can't believe this. We're being bullied by a gang of pre-pubescent peasants. I smile at the alliterative nature of that term. Pre-pubescent peasants. Say it fast. Prepubescentpeasants. PPBP. Still, they're basically children, just looking around here I can see that they have bugger all to entertain themselves. I'm the same at home. I consider my own life, and I get

the greatest, funniest light-bulb moment I've ever
had. They might have strength in numbers but I've
just had an idea.

"Whatta thar fuckin' smilin' at suvvern wanker?"
Greasy face asks me, I actually understood that one.
I'm learning already. Pulling himself to as near to toe-
to-toe as he can, considering he's less than five feet
and I'm six foot one, the PPBP pushes his forehead
into my chest, like the world's worst stag. I chance
my arm.

"Do you want to see something funny?" I ask, which
works slightly in deflating our young hero. His
friends are already curious, and my question has
attracted positive nods from most of them. Greasy
face pulls away.

"What? Funnier than your fuckin' face?" he asks,
turning to his gathered crew, sniggering, serving to
remind me that he's about ten.

"Yes, funnier than my fucking face. Do you want to
see it?" I feel my confidence rising still, and I *just*
know that they're going to love this. By now they're
all nodding all slack jawed and eager. Danny's looking
at me, and I turn to look back, and nod.

"Okay," I say, "Danny, punch yourself in the face."

***

The atmosphere in the Bentley is subdued on our
way back down the M1. The Johnny Cash CD finished
about two hours ago and Danny hasn't thought to
restart it, which is fine by me. I can see his eyes
flicker to register me in the rear-view mirror every
now.

"Do you have anything to say Danny?" I call from the
back, swirling the last of the champagne around the
base of the flute, he thinks about saying something

but then holds back. He's *not* a happy bunny, "That was really quite fun in the end!" I continue, goading him into a response but he's failing to play the game. Perhaps I went slightly too far but *for God's sake,* he threw himself out of a window not yesterday for my entertainment. What's so different about what *I* did?

"You didn't have to do that," he says quietly, but reasonably audible.

"Do what?" I ask, quite innocently.

"You know," he says into the rear-view mirror.

"Oh, come on it was funny, you're always hurting yourself for money, and I thought you'd appreciate the break."

He really does seem rather cross.

"You set twenty kids on me for money Fintan!" he roars into the rear-view, and I'm rather worried that he's forgetting that he's driving, "What kind of friend pays to get their friend beaten unconscious for fun?!" I consider this. Are we friends? He's just a man that showed up on our doorstep one day and never left. He's more like a household pe-

-Time slows down as I'm thrown from my seat amidst a cacophony of noise. A squealing, screeching, clanging noise. The champagne bottle smashes around my head as I'm sailing forward. The crushed rear end of the car in front of us draws nearer and nearer to my head. My body rotates one hundred and eighty degrees and the ceiling of the Bentley is my view. Another ninety degrees and my face passes Danny's. He's looking directly into my eyes, his hands gripped so tight around the seat belt he has strapped around his stupid stupid torso that they are almost pure white, and I couldn't be one hundred per cent positive on this, but I'm *sure* the last thing he does is mouth the word 'cunt'.

THE HAPPIEST DAY OF YOUR LIVES

"Ladies and gentlemen, if I could just grab a few minutes of your precious time," I say, tinkling the glass with the side of a spoon. For sure, I'm feeling proper professional and that, "people! People!" There's a shitload of mumbling. People settling down to hear my words. Others are telling their mates to be quiet. Then eventually it gets to be as quiet as I could probably expect it to be, and I clear my throat. Been looking forward to this bit all day. I've done my usual best man tasks. Given the rings out, sorted the photos, made sure my boy has a nice amount of confidence up his nose. That kind of thing. The ceremony was spot on, given the circumstances, just the right amount of tears of joy. Some of anguish for the missing brother. I didn't let it get to me much, I always thought he was a prick. I'm sure he'll turn up. "Okay, people, ladies and gentlemen. It's a great honour to be here performing these tasks for my great and true friend Dicko. I mean, Lee. For sure, he's an absolute gentleman in every sense of the word. I've known him years. Longer infect. There's no boy on Earth that I'd rather be the best man for. Apart from maybe Johnny Marr, but he's not here." A few titters from those with an ounce of musical knowledge, but for the most part intent on letting me say my thing.

"I'll always remember when Lee came up to me and told me that he thought he'd met the woman of his dreams. I laughed my arse off, I really did, because he's always been a warm 'un. Can't keep it in his pants. Well, he *couldn't* keep it in his pants," I say, noting a few looks of disapproval, "until he met the beautiful Fiona."

I smile down at the bride, she's not impressed with me, but that's fine. I'm the best man. The *best* man. She'll get over it.

"Fiona whirled into his life like a hurricane. A beautiful, sexy, stunner of a hurricane. He was besotted by her. I can tell you. There were so many times I asked him if he was coming up the town and he said no. You know why ladies and gentlemen? You know why? Because he was head over heels in love with her. She's *so* good for him. He-"

I pause. Aware that I'm going off on one. I *knew* I should've left the coke out of the party, at least until the speech was done, can't help myself though, can I?

"She is. She's great for him. She's made a real man out of my favourite boy. I'm gonna miss him, of course I am. Much like a lot of you are missing Tony."

My mouth feels dry, and I grab a sip of water. Some people have just broken down over the missing brother, but like I say, he'll show up. For sure, he's a grown man, he can disappear anytime he wants. It was a bit weird how he just vanished like. For sure, if I end up being one of the last people to see him alive I'll be annoyed. I'm supposed to be working a new job, they'll go off their nut if I start getting time off work to answer police questions and that. Selfish cunt that he is. Dicko is looking at me like I've just done a shit in his top hat for that last remark. I pat his shoulder, I've got this covered.

"Our prayers and thoughts are all with Tony right now, wherever he is."

I catch the eye of Dicko's mum Theresa right about now, she's having a little chuckle to herself. She knows I'm fucking this up royally, but I also know that she can't stand Tony. Or *couldn't* stand him. If he's dead like. She flashes me a wink. I smile. Always loved flirting with her. Dicko hates it. I'd never do owt about it though. It's my mate's mum. For sure, she's right off-limits. It's not just that though. My dick is still sore. I snapped my banjo string the other week on a fit student in Leeds. Still a bit sore whenever I get a stiffy. My balls are fit for bursting, I can tell you. "The bridesmaids are looking gorgeous. Little Sophie and her big sister Janice."
The bridesmaids are *not* looking gorgeous. Little Sophie is quite cute, as far as eight year olds with violent eczema go, and her big sister Janice. Well, let's just say she's definitely her *big* sister. Rolls of lard billowing out of every hole in that dress. It's like a play dough fun factory, but with fire damage. I smile though. I hold the glass up.
"To the bridesmaids," I say, and the room repeats it, "and to the mother of the bride, even though she must be going off her nut with Tony missing and that, she's looking as elegant as ever. Mrs Grimbleby everyone."
The room is split on this one, because she's just broken down in tears. Missing her boy I'd guess. He was thirty odd and still lived with her. She did everything for him, or so I'm told. I carry on, undeterred.
"To the beautiful Mrs Dickinson, Theresa, you created a fantastic boy here," I ruffle Dicko's hair, much to his annoyance, "he is my hero. Theresa everyone!"
Glasses go up some more, and I carry this speech on in much the same vein. For sure, I think I did a great

job, but a lot of people are looking a bit mumpy with me for bringing Tony up all the time.

Once the speeches and dinners are out of the way, it's that kind of lull between them and the night do, where everybody's a bit unsure on how best to entertain themselves. Not that I ate much of my dinner. Cocaine kills the appetite don't you know. Dicko and his lovely wife Fiona have gone upstairs to their hotel room to do a bit of whatever, and I'm downstairs holding court with some of the guests, including Mrs Theresa Dickinson.
"Oh Tom, that was hilarious, really good speech, well done," she smiles, leaning in to me. I'm *sure* she rubs one of her tits against my arm on purpose, and I don't move it, even though I suppose I should.
"Cheers Mrs D," I say gratefully, "I were a bit nervous to start with, but once I got into it it were child's play."
"When you kept mentioning Tony, it was priceless. They were in bits."
Now, I'm *sure* she's flirting with me now, because she's licking her lips a bit, and she does this thing where she leans over to grab something, and one of her tits *definitely* rubs the back of my hand. I can't handle this. I can feel blood swirling around my body but being pulled down toward my injured cock like as if it were a blood magnet. And she's my mate's mum, for fuck's sake. I pull back just slightly, and she does this really slow wink with her left eye. I think she must be a bit tipsy. I decide that a nice fat line of coke is just the ticket I need out of this potentially awkward situation, so I make my excuses and head for the bogs. She's looking a bit deflated, and I feel bad, because for sure, she's fit as fuck for an older woman. But she's my mate's mum.

I'm in the bogs and I'm racking up a double hit of charlie to clear my head. This is probably not the best idea because sometimes I get horny as fuck, but it doesn't matter, I need self-control. I need to harness every inch of self-control I ever had and put it into the effort of resisting the sexy Mrs Theresa Dickinson. The lines are demolished and I mooch back into the hotel bar. Some other people have disappeared back to their rooms, and it's only a few left down there, including, and I can't help being attracted to her centre of gravity, Mrs Theresa Dickinson.

"Thought you'd binned me off," she chuckles, and I'm thinking binned me off? Who the fuck says that? Maybe it's a generational thing.

"Nah, no chance Mrs D, fittest woman in the place you," I say, instantly regretting the words because her eyes light up.

"Do you want to go back to my room?" she asks, and I have to play this one very carefully, because I don't want to let her down harshly like. For sure, I've known her years, it could make for very uncomfortable meetings in the future, "just for a drink, of course," she clarifies, which, in my head seems fine. Drinks it is.

"Just for a drink," I say, "of course."

So we're walking into her room, and I have to say, on first glance I don't see any drinks. Just a bag in the corner. I turn to her to express this concern when she's at me like a bull. Her lips clashing against mine, and I want to stop it, but I can't. She's surprisingly powerful is Mrs D, so I just go with it. I let her lead the way and we enjoy a good two hours of what can only be described as wrongness.

The evening do comes round, and I'm back downstairs. I've just nailed half a gram of cocaine in the toilets and I'm jabbering away at anybody who'll listen. I'm talking music, and dancing, and festivals, and drugs. My balls are several pounds lighter, but my dick is in real pain. I'm sure Mrs D took my gasps of pain to be gasps of enjoyment because she's thrashed the shit of me. For sure, she's a lively one. Dicko approaches me as I'm adjusting my cock in discomfort. He looks smart as hell in his suit. I'm proud of the boy.

"Banjo giving you grief lad?" he asks, and I'm suddenly feeling guilty as fuck, because the next thing I say, and I promise you I don't mean to, it just comes out, is "Yeah, your mum really knows how to fuck. It's a good job you can't snap it twice."

Dicko's laughing at this. I mean, really laughing, because he knows what I'm like, I talk some right shit, only, the thing is, his mum comes up to us literally two seconds later and says, "thanks for that earlier Tom, I really needed it."

I don't remember the rest of the night, given that I got ten bells of shit kicked out of me. Needless to say, Dicko never spoke to me again.

THE BANJO STRING SNAPPED
BUT THE BAND PLAYED ON

See my tambourine
Ain't no funki tangerine
I will bang it
In your face
And I will draw blood
From your skull
And I will watch you
Drown in your own vomit.

That's why I like you.

Campag Velocet – Ain't no Funki Tangerine

Lyrics used with the kind permission
of Pete Voss

Jesus and The Pimp

Sometime in 2006. Saturday. Ten in the morning.

Jesus didn't speak. Just sat, slumped on the green and red padded and striped bench behind the knackered old table, the remains of a beer mat bunched up in a small pile of shredded card from where he'd decimated it. His filthy, muddy, blood stained previously-white trainers poked their scabby noses out from beneath his torn piss-stained robe. His crown of thorns was a distant memory, as was his makeshift crucifix, only the faded red stigmata remained of his sacrifice to humankind. His bright red-rimmed eyelids battled gravity bravely but felt so heavy. His neck felt as if it had been chipped away at by an invisible lumberjack, and was now holding on to his ten-stone head by luck alone. He needed to sleep. He'd give up everything he owned, or had ever owned, to be in his bed right now. Through his glassy eyed gaze he watched The Pimp approach, his own shitty feeling mirrored in The Pimp's demeanour. The Pimp clumsily plonked the pint glasses down onto the table, spilling ice cold cider over his fingers, the beer mats, and the sticky chipped varnish of the wooden surface. The Pimp pulled his wet fingers to his mouth and slurped the booze from them with a laboured effort. The last thing Jesus needed now was more drink, so he was more than surprised by his own hand's actions as it sailed through the air toward the pint glass, returning to his proximity with the booze, drawing it to his lips which surprised him further still by gulping down a generous helping. The alcohol burned his throat, and did absolutely nothing to quench the raging thirst which had been a product of his weekend so far, he would happily kill for a massive glass of water, lemonade, Coke, anything. Anything that did not have an alcohol content. Had a random stranger entered the bar, and handed him a machine gun with the instruction to pepper each and every one of the locals in their stupid faces in exchange for a two-litre bottle of lemonade he would have undertaken his deadly task with a veritable relish, and only when he'd absorbed every drop of thirst quenching goodness would the guilt over his merciless killing spree begin to set in. *But at least I'd not be thirsty*, he thought malevolently. The Pimp still hadn't spoken to him, they both remained in their own bubbles of self-loathing, exhaustion, and just good old agony. Jesus felt a shooting pain whisk from beneath the tip of his cock, down the shaft and rush past his balls, forcing his arsehole to clench so tight it could snap a pencil. It would definitely need looking at.

The Pimp didn't notice his friend's discomfort, he was watching the back of an old man, seated beside his trusty Labrador. On any other day he'd probably be up there, crouching to stroke the dog, giving it the daft voice, patting the old lad on the belly. The dog, not the owner. Today, however, he wanted to drag the wretched thing through the door and tie it to a railing, or boot it home, anything to get that aroma of its wet stinking coat from the back of his throat, attacking his drug ravaged sinuses with a vengeance. The Pimp didn't want to be here any more than his friend did but here they were. He was adorned from top to toe in bright purple velour. In contrast to his caveman resembling friend The Pimp had retained his headgear, the bright purple pimp hat complete with peacock feather tucked in the hat strap. His zebra print collars remained intact too but would undoubtedly need to be dry-cleaned before he returned it. The seat of his trousers was crusted with something that he'd eaten, and subsequently sat upon at some point in the last twenty four hours. The pair continued to sit, and stare, until Jesus broke the silence.

"Am fucked."

"Me an'all," The Pimp offered, it seemed like much too much effort to go on. Jesus nodded in acknowledgment.

"Proper fucked," he muttered, pulling the half drained glass to his lips once more. This cider was supposed to be refreshing, but it was fighting a losing battle with his fur lined tongue and teeth, which felt like they hadn't experienced the fantastic sensation of being brushed in days, and his taste buds were buried so deep into the scum in his mouth that they may as well not exist. Jesus sighed.

"Fiona's gonna gimme a right kickin'," The Pimp said, before struggling through a sticky, tight, painful swallow of what little moisture was left in his mouth. Jesus didn't turn to look at him, but he wholeheartedly agreed.

"It'll be reyt," he said, closing his eyes for what could quite easily have been the ten millionth time since they trudged into the pub, attracting amused glances and smirking comments. This time they really didn't want to open, his body felt like it was very much shutting down. Game over, the final whistle had been blown, injury time had been played and had expired long ago.

"If yer gonna fall asleep get yerself home Jesus!"

His eyes slowly opened. George, the landlord of the establishment was directing this demand his way. Jesus pulled the last of the pint of cider into his throat and turned to The Pimp.

"Reckon that's me then mate, for sure, I could sleep for a week," said Jesus, rocking unsteadily on his feet, the rush of blood to the help not helping his fragile state any. The Pimp looked up to his comrade, and let out a foul tasting, foul smelling burp. Jesus smiled, as he was easily amused by such comedy, and shook his head, "that fuckin' stinks."

The Pimp returned the exhausted smile.

"See yer int week mate," he said, as he watched the back of Jesus retreat to the door of the pub, "Tom!" he called. Jesus turned to face him, "fuckin' brilliant night mate, honestly, mad as fuck. Best best man ever. Cheers," he declared, holding up the last of his own pint in honour of Jesus, who slowly and labouredly saluted The Pimp.

"Proper mad as fuck. See yer int week brother."

When The Pimp reopened his eyes the door had closed behind his pal. He shook his head almost in disbelief. The weekend started on Friday, like many good weekends should. There had been Jesus, The Pimp, Superman, two smurfs, The Incredible Hulk, Beetlejuice, Hitler, Al Capone, and Bungle from Rainbow. Come ten o'clock this Saturday morning, however, their numbers had diminished for a variety of reasons, and they were the last two standing. Jesus and The Pimp. What a pair. As he swallowed the last of his pint he smiled a slow, and satisfied smile.

Three days ago

Wednesday. Five past eleven.

Name: Tom
Age: 24
Occupation: Unemployed
Likes: Music & women
Dislikes: People who use unnecessarily long words
Most Likely to Dance to: Campag Velocet – Ain't No Funki Tangerine

I'm sitting in an open plan waiting area, my fingers tapping impatiently on the arm of the low sofa I'm parked in. There are massive potted trees all over the place, it's like they've turned the Amazon rainforest into a crisp, clean, clinical waiting room. There's a big circular reception desk, with two middle aged bags who tend to everybody that approaches their centre of gravity. I'd smiled at the saggiest of the pair with my butter-wouldn't-melt best effort at a smile, as genuine as I could muster like, but she returned my serve with the stoniest killer glare as she slid the visitor book my way. Honestly, it were like I'd fucked her last week and given her the marching orders while I'm still in the process of shooting me muck up her weathered back. She looked at me with that much vitriol. I've been waiting here for about twenty minutes. For sure, first impressions do not bode well here. I know I'm supposed to be here to impress these cunts with my sparkling wit and charm, but let's be fair, it's a two way street. I'm supposed to want to work here. I fucking hate waiting for stuff. Food in a restaurant does my head in, especially if I see someone who got served after me get their snap

before me. Honestly, does my fucking head in. I hate
waiting in a pub queue for exactly the same reason. I
used to be one of them who'd point at somebody
who'd been waiting before I got there, in the hope
that the barman would notice my adherence to the
etiquette, but they rarely did. No, I'd be standing
there with my thumb up my arse, having given some
jammy cunt the green light on ordering his drinks,
then the wanker of a barman would trundle off down
the other end of the bar and I'm left waiting for
another half an hour till I got my order in. Not any
more, for sure, it's dog eat dog pal, I'm telling you.
Every man for himself. I digress, and I'm still waiting
for my interviewer. Two blondies come in from
having a ciggie together and I catch the eye of the
best looking of the pair, delivering to her a cheeky
smile first class special delivery. She turns to her
mate and giggles a bit, throwing me another glance
before they disappear through the turnstile and out
of my life. I sigh, quite loudly, as if this is gonna make
the battered old bag behind the desk speed things up
somewhat. My watch says it's almost ten past eleven,
the letter in front of me says to come for my
interview for eleven o'clock, and I've been here since
quarter to. Poor show Electric Company, poor show
indeed.
Eventually some kid comes shuffling through, looking
all sheepish and apologetic, but beaming a smile my
way.
"Tom?" he asks, and I nod and drag my bones upright
and over to him. His clammy weak handshake
crumbles in my firm man's grip, like he's been dead
for centuries and his bones have basically turned to
dust, but they're still in shape until they're disturbed,
and they crumble to nothing. That's how weak his

handshake is, but neither of us mentions it, "I'm Martin, do you want to come through?"

We're walking side by side along a brightly lit corridor, rooms and doors pass us on both sides, and I can see Martin is itching to make small talk but I'm still a bit annoyed with him for keeping me waiting, so I'm fucked if I'm gonna throw him a bone on this one. I could go in with something about the weather, the decor, the sheer size of this place. I could go in with that fit blonde girl, tell him I my observation that this place is packed to the rafters with top notch Grade A fanny, but he can whistle, I'm saying nowt!

He stops at a door and opens it to reveal a small table with three chairs surrounding it. Filling one of the chairs is another blonde, she's slightly older than those from the lobby, but no less fit. Her hair's long as fuck, and really full, and it frames her elegant looking face and high cheek bones. She smiles at me but doesn't get up, but then why would she? I'm not royalty or owt! I smile back, she's a very welcome alternative to our Martin here. Martin looks like he's been here since he left school, and had attained a position of authority by default. His suit looks slightly just too big, his little digits poking out of the end of the sleeves, grasped tightly around the forms as if they were the meaning of life itself. In stark contrast, this newcomer to the situation looks a cut above, for sure, she looks like she shits golden nuggets, she's carrying herself that well, and she's wearing her tank top on and suit trousers really well. On first impression I think she's pretty cool, she holds the eye contact much better than the boy Martin. She's got class, but at the same time I think she would definitely know what to do with a cock if you put it in front of her. We'll see eh?

"Take a seat," she says, I don't know if her eyes are flirting with me yet, but I'll find out, she's getting all of my attention today.

"Thanks."

I park the arse and sit up, back straight, hands on the table. Standard procedure. Martin joins the girl, they look at me, and I look back.

"This is Lynsey," says Martin, and I'm holding the hand out to greet this divine piece of fluff. She graciously accepts it and smiles, and I'm thinking I'm glad I'm seated, cause I'm pitching a trouser tent just now.

"Hi," I say, still not taking my eye off of her, not in a sleazy way, no, I'm just trying to dig into her soul, plant a seed of attraction, and water that bad boy. Eventually she slides her hand from mine, and looks to the young lad to start the show.

"So," he says, looking back down to the application form, searching for my name, "Tom, did you find us okay?"

I nod, and clear my throat.

"Yeah, thank you."

That's enough with the small talk, let's get down to business.

"Good, good. So, tell me about yourself, what do you like to do?"

So here's where we're at, we've got what Actual Tom likes to get up to, and then there's what Interview Tom likes to get up to.

What Actual Tom gets up to:

I amble through life doing pretty much whatever I feel like. I won't turn a night out down because I'm scared of missing out on anything. Whether that anything could include a line of coke that I might be gifted by a mate who surprises me in the pisser of some back alley pub, or bumping into a bird who might accept my advances and let me empty my balls onto her tits before the end of the night. And. Just those, to be honest. I have no other aims in life. For sure, I have other hobbies, like gigs, and films, and playing Xbox with my mates with a cocktail of drugs between us, arguing the toss over whether we should stick with Fifa or move on to something a bit more intense like Halo. I have no strong political views. For the most part I'll leave you alone if you leave me alone, but I still have a strong sense of justice and I'm not scared to stick up for the small man if I think you're taking the piss. I've fucked a lot of birds, I don't remember many of their names, but I know for a fact I've had three Sarahs, three Andreas, and two Laurens. I've not duplicated any more names, they're all unique. Some more unique than others, Sharanne, for example. These are what, and who Actual Tom likes to do.

What Interview Tom gets up to:

"I'm a big music fan, so I enjoy attending gigs, watching some up and coming bands especially. I wish I had the skills to play an instrument well, but I don't so I really enjoy watching the professionals, live vicariously through them you know?"
Martin's nodding in agreement, Lynsey's smiling.
"I'm really into writing too, I really like to give my imagination a work out, and so whether it's poetry or a short story, I'm like a pig in-"
I stop myself here, rolling my eyes, and it gives cue to a gasp from Martin.
"Sorry, I got carried away, let's just say I'm very happy when I'm giving my brain a work out."

Everybody laughs now. Well played Thomas my boy, well played.

"But seriously, I always like to be busy, I love learning things. I hate not knowing something so if I can't do something, I will work harder and harder until I can do it, maybe it's a curse, but that's just how I am."

I look to the beautiful Lynsey with a smile in my eyes. Martin's head is rocking back and forth all sage-like, as if he sees a kindred spirit in me. No chance pal. I'm just mainlining smoke directly up into your arse.

"I know what you're saying, I'm exactly the same," he purrs, and I'm thinking I really fucking doubt that pal but my face doesn't betray the emotion, "so why do you want to work for Electric Company?"

"I want to make a difference, so many times have I called up my energy supplier and been treated like I'm nothing. I want to show the public that they're people and not just numbers. For sure, a customer is the lifeblood of any business. A customer shouldn't be an interruption of our work, a customer *is* our work."

Now there's not just me with a trouser tent in the room, Martin is looking at me like I'm made of tits, and Lynsey, I dunno, I think she knows I'm talking utter bollocks but at the same time she's not knocking my performance. Far from it. If I had to guess, I'd say she was a smart girl, and she knows exactly what these places are all about, I bet she keeps her cards close to her chest. I've worked in enough of them to know exactly what they want to hear, which is precisely what I tell them, all the while talking to this Lynsey girl with my eyes. When she's telling me with her mouth that I'll be notified within twenty four hours, I'm telling her with my eyes that she can abuse the system if she wants, grab my number from the file and text me any time. She won't though. Far too cool for that shit. No, I can play the long game, I mean, for sure this job is nailed on, it's only a matter of getting in here and putting the charmers on her at a later date.

I'm out of there about half an hour later and sparking up a ciggie, feeling extremely good about my chances. I'd put on a top notch performance, sang all the right notes, said all the right stuff, and now I can forget about it for a bit. I've got my boy Dicko's stag do this weekend, and as the best man it's my responsibility to make sure he forgets more than he remembers. His bird, Fiona, his lovely wife to be, she's a bit of a warm 'un, so I need to behave myself a little bit or she'll knock my teeth out, but come on, it's his fucking stag do. He's getting the works!

Friday. Five thirty in the afternoon.

"Lads! Minibus is here!" Jesus calls from the door, beckoning the rest of his band of fearless adventurers to finish their drinks. Hitler and Beetlejuice stand by the front door, the pair of them are sucking the arses out of their cigarettes, hoping to beat the rest of them to the minibus, thus securing seats in the back, rather than up front beside the toothless driver. The Incredible Hulk and Superman clamber into the bus, followed by Al Capone. Jesus steals a few drags from Hitler's cigarette before he's done with it.

"You get sorted with the pills?" Jesus asks of Hitler, who responds with a nodded affirmation, and is treated to an appreciative pat on the back from his friend, "good lad."

One by one the team assemble upon the bus. The Incredible Hulk, Superman, and Al Capone on the back seats. Up in front of them The Pimp, Jesus, and Hitler. Directly behind the driver are the Smurfs and Beetlejuice, which, since he'd been in the toilets chopping up an early line of charlie, and then climbing back into his suit, left the unfortunate Bungle from Rainbow up front. The driver is long and thin, his knees knock together at chest height since he has been forced to pull his seat forward as far as it will go to allow for the unfeasibly tall smurf that resides behind him, his yellowed twiglet fingers wrap themselves tightly around the steering wheel. His eyes flicker to the rear view mirror, and he seems to be of the understanding that he'll be liaising directly with Jesus.

"Leeds then yeah?" he asks, knowing full well that Leeds is indeed the destination for the trip. The cream of society cheer in unison, drowning out the religious icon, then a sharp hiss and crack echoes from the back of the bus, and Superman slurps enthusiastically on his tin of lager. Beside him, tucked down behind the seats so as not to attract the attention of the human stick insect that drives the vehicle, The Incredible Hulk has created a clumsy, fat line of cocaine on the back of the cash card that Al Capone holds as steadily as he can. At this moment at least one of the pair is fantasising that this exercise is a game on some nineties game show, where The Incredible Hulk must snort the whole line under duress, and a thirty second time limit, and his friend must hold the surface steady. If the line is finished successfully then they might win a caravan, or a selection of kitchen appliances. He wishes that Jim, Bowen or Davidson, he's not fussy which one, were watching over them, cracking innuendo laden jokes, geeing up the audience who are cheering the tenacious heroes on. The Incredible Hulk expertly despatches the drugs up into his hooter, and looks to Al Capone gratefully, his glassy eyes blinking a small tear away. On the three seats in front of them Jesus is up on his knees.

"Lads, it's fifteen quid a piece, come on, get yer cash out!" he instructs them, holding his miniature crucifix aloft with one hand, and the crown of thorns atop his head. The nine heads tilt simultaneously as each of them reaches into whichever pocket to retrieve the taxi fare.

"Nah mate, it's your fucking stag do, keep yer money in yer pocket," Hitler informs The Pimp with a gentle hand rested on his arm. The Pimp is thankful of this reprieve, as it's fifteen quid which could definitely go to better use later today, probably on two minutes with an Eastern European lap dancer grinding her sweaty crotch against his, desperately trying to pump some more life into his cock, enough that he'll scrabble around his pockets for another tenner when the generic dance tune ends, she'll be about to pull up her sequin lined G-string, and then he'll spend that tenner on two more minutes of her time. All the while he'll be trying to stare into her cold dead eyes, see if he can't stir any kind of emotion other than raw indifference, something that will make him feel like he's a cut above the rest of the sleazy fuckers that frequent the place more often than he does.

Jesus collects the money from the boys, and tots it up. He's fifteen quid short. For the briefest of seconds he doesn't trust a single one of these people on board the taxi, one of them is trying to dodge the fare. Of all the dirty cheeky cunt things to do, he thinks, before suddenly realising that he is the one who hasn't paid yet. He was so busy collecting that he'd forgotten to stump up the dough himself. Jesus is thankful that he'd not embarrassed himself by declaring a random one of his friends a tight cunt. He eyes the back of Beetlejuice's head almost apologetically, as he is ashamed to admit that Beetlejuice was going to be his first port of call with the good ship blame.

Beetlejuice, unaware of the slight mental betrayal of Jesus, is talking to Big Poppa Smurf.

"Mate, she were all over me, honestly, she'd have sucked us off right there if I'd let her."

Big Poppa Smurf looks doubtfully at Beetlejuice, who has never been known for his sexual prowess or his attractiveness to the opposite sex, but Beetlejuice is looking deadly serious, almost like he can't believe the accusation against the unnamed woman himself, who is probably somewhere pouring ice cold water over her burning ears to cool the fire.

"Get fucked yer daft cunt," laughs Big Poppa Smurf, inciting a hurt look from the undead prankster, but Big Poppa Smurf isn't finished, "'ere lads! Who saw this daft cunt rattin' birds last week? Did anyone see this bird that he's talkin' about? Did she have a white stick?" he laughs loudly, and derisively. There's the rabble of noises of agreement that Beetlejuice could fall in a barrel of tits and still come out of there sucking a cock. The unfortunate front-riding Bungle turns to face the rest of them, his fat fuzzy head scraping against the ceiling of the van.

"I saw her, honestly mate, I wunt touch her wi' yours," he says to The Pimp, "she looked like she'd scraped herself off the road after bein' hit by a truck, our Ellie had more teeth than her!"

Beetlejuice rides out the inevitable barrage of friendly abuse, all the while hoping that the attention directed his way is diverted sooner rather than later. They're all mates so he likes to appear to take it in good humour, but the reality of it is that it makes him really uncomfortable, his cheeks betray his discomfort and glow pink beneath the white face paint. The rough hand of Jesus ruffles his pale grey wig, dislodging the thing slightly.

By the time the taxi is on the motorway headed north, the gang are in full swing, Superman and The Incredible Hulk are roaring football terrace songs, pulling Al Capone into their embrace. Jesus is talking ten to the dozen to The Pimp about the line-up for the Leeds Festival this year.

"Yeah but last thing you want on a Friday night when you're off yer chops at Leeds is Franz fuckin' Ferdinand, y'know?" he says, but The Pimp isn't listening properly, as his attention is also being held by King Smurf, who is unscrewing the cap of his small bottle of vodka, and taking a harsh but generous gulp of the liquid, before passing it back to The Pimp, who does the same. The Pimp's face creases out of all recognition as the burning bitter flavour attacks every part of his mouth and throat.

"I mean, Primal Scream is miles better, what's wrong wi' dumpin' Franz fuckin' Ferdinand on that stage and promotin' a decent band to the main stage?" Jesus is continuing, The Pimp nods through the vodka burn, and feels a gassy bubble roll up from his stomach, and up his throat. For comedy value The Pimp captures the belch in his cheeks, before blowing the foul smelling gas into the face of Hitler.

"You dirty cunt!" Hitler wafts with vigour, trying in vain to remove the stink from his vicinity, The Pimp snorts with laughter. He is having the time of his life. He has nine of his best mates on a minibus to Leeds, he's getting married to the girl of his dreams in little over a week's time, and between them they have enough drugs to kill Hunter S. Thompson. At that exact precise moment, The Pimp is feeling very, very content.

Hitler
Real Name: Dean 'Dizzy' Retford
Age: 26
Occupation: Roofer
Likes: Sheffield United & the gym
Dislikes: Sheffield Wednesday & rainy weather
Most Likely to Dance to: Sisqo - The Thong Song

The minibus pulls up by the railway station at about six thirty as instructed, and Hitler is the first to the sliding door, jumping from the vehicle. The van had been filled to the brim with the raucous sound of ten increasingly drunken characters, and the sound of the city traffic serves almost as a welcome release from the claustrophobic vehicle. The rest of the crew pile from the taxi as Hitler regards his reflection in the window. His 'tache is still stuck firm, but the swastika armband has bunched up slightly, so his eager fingers pick at the edging and straighten the controversial icon against the twitching muscle of his right bicep. Hitler is a very clean, very well kept bloke. His flat is a minimalist psychologist's dream. Because he spends three hours every morning in the gym he is conscious of his alcohol intake, he drinks only occasionally, on special occasions such as this. He does, however, enjoy a chemical supper. The MDMA that he'd dropped in the taxi is beginning to take a hold of his senses, and the city of Leeds is looking very vibrant to him. The crooked cross of the swastika has never looked so evocative. His friends are the best people on Earth. His attention is drawn to the grand architecture of the Queen's Hotel which backs on to the railway station. The huge, pale building with its potted flowers-

"Dizzy!" Jesus calls to him from the pedestrian crossing, "you comin' or what mate?"

Hitler smiles and turns to face the group before him, nine icons all out to celebrate the impending nuptials of the purple clad Pimp, and heads over to them as the green man blinks and they cross the road, and the first bar of many is already in their sights. The general public part before them without fail, there's nobody in the city that wants to get in the way of the novelty, ten-headed behemoth from Sheffield. The gang are in high spirits, and still relatively sober.

"You're a top fella you mate," says Hitler to The Incredible Hulk, and he means it too. He hooks his considerable arm around his friend's neck like an Anaconda and pulls him closer, whispers into his ear, "honestly mate, best fuckin' bloke I know."

The Incredible Hulk looks grateful of Hitler's sentiment, but his head feels as if it's in danger of popping from his neck as if it were a novelty ice cream toy with the pop-off foam ball, bought from some market in Cleethorpes in the nineties, so he wrenches himself from the grasp of the nazi leader, and slaps a firm green hand on his back.

"You an'all mate, you're a right boy," says The Incredible Hulk, as they enter the pub. Jesus is already up ordering the shots, and the rest are scattered across the bar in small groups. Superman is served so Hitler sees his chance, and sidles up alongside him.

"Get us a pint in Jimmy," he says, slipping the blue and red hero a fiver and craning his muscular neck to see the selection available to him, "get us a wife beater," he confirms. Although he doesn't drink often, when he does he likes to make it a good one, so Stella Artois is the only way for him.

The pub itself is quiet for this time of day, as the last of the older, weather beaten, predominantly unemployed day-drinkers are slowly filtering out, to be replaced by the fresher, younger, and altogether more affluent night-drinkers. A dubstep CD plays from the speakers at a palatable volume, but the bulky, cloth covered DJ booth in the corner not so much hints as it does screams at the prospect of a livelier time to come. The stairs to the first floor are roped off and Hitler is already considering this place for a possible return later on, thinks about putting it to The Pimp, but he becomes sidetracked by Al Capone at the bandit. It's a Deal or No Deal gambler, and Al Capone has managed to win his way on to play the feature game.

"No deal! No deal!" Hitler calls to the gangster as he approaches, without seeing which values that he still has available to him. Al Capone doesn't respond, his focus is very much on the potential jackpot if he plays it right. Hitler and Capone don't generally run in the same circles, but they are aware of each other. Hitler, on any other day, could happily pass Al Capone in the street and perhaps not even nod a greeting to the bloke, but today his brain is fizzing with MDMA, with the general good feeling and love that comes with it. He wants Al Capone to win jackpot more than he wants anything. His jaw is tensing, and his teeth are already grinding gently together.

"He's gonna do it!" he calls to anybody that will listen, Al Capone is doing well, he is down to only two boxes, four quid, and the jackpot, the offer from the tiny banker inside the machine is thirty two quid. Hitler is willing him on, to make a heavy display of big balls and press the no deal. Capone chews his gum, and contemplates the offer, but Hitler is eager, he wants to press the no deal button. He is far too excited right now, he actually thinks he's in the TV studio. Noel's face beams out from the display before them.

Capone's finger floats up and is headed for the deal button. Hitler, through the positive vibes, is disappointed. He thinks Capone should take the gamble. Before he knows it Hitler has taken the decision out of Capone's hands. His finger is firmly pressed over the button which will decline the very generous offer.

"What you fuckin' playin' at? Eh? Dickhead?" Al Capone bellows in his face. Al is not a small bloke either, and he pushes his forehead firmly into that of Hitler, who is smiling and unfazed.

"Chill out mate, have faith," he says, a handful of the group are already advising Capone that he needs to calm down, that he's in danger of spoiling the night already and they've only been in Leeds for ten minutes. More of the group have circled them now, hands pat at them, and try to hold arms back despite the fact that no punches look to be pulled any time soon. The bar staff are on red alert, and the lone doorman, a small wiry looking nutcase, covered from the head down in home-made tattoos watches from afar. He is a coiled spring, itching for a release trigger so that he can pounce into the unsuspecting group with his bony ring-clad knuckles swinging. Hitler still grins his Cheshire Cat smile as Capone stands toe to toe with him, he's thoroughly convinced that he's done the right thing, but with the way he's feeling, even if Capone spits the dummy out of the pram even further, and wants to fight, Hitler will not. Today he is a lover, and not a fighter. The theme tune of Deal or No Deal plays loudly, the lights flash, Noel's eyes blink rapidly with green, red, yellow, and white lights. Capone has won the jackpot.

***

He's a bit of a strange one that Tony. I mean, for sure he looks the business in his gangster get up, the pure white trilby hat and the tommy gun, the black shirt with the white *Rock On Tommy* bracers, but he's not a real gangster and he's just properly overreacted. It seems our Dizzy's not just pushed his button in the literal sense. Yeah, for sure, he seems to have pushed his massive, and seemingly easy to find, irritation button. We'll see how we're feeling, I might have some fun with that later. He's Fiona's brother, I only invited him 'cause she was pecking my head about it, *Are you gonna invite our Tony? You ARE inviting our Tony aren't ya Tom? You can't NOT invite our Tony!* and I was thinking, *I fucking can, and I fucking will NOT invite your Tony* and then we were out at The Oak one night and she's there, then Tony's there, you know? So she sees her opportunity to make it very fucking difficult to get out of without looking like a complete cunt. *So when's the stag do Tom?* She says, all sly 'cause she knows *exactly* when his fucking stag do is, so I'm having to kinda backtrack and act like I sent him a Facebook invite, and start joking about how some other random Tony Grimbleby will show up on the minibus 'cause I sent it to the wrong bloke. I don't think he bought it, I don't even think he wanted to come, but here he is, squaring up to my mates. Dizzy's off his tits like, gurning like fuck and it's only seven o'clock, needs to pace himself, and I know he can be a bit overbearing sometimes but let's face it, it's *his* mates he's out with. If Tony wants to start squaring up to every cunt in the gang he'll find himself very hurt, and it'll be very quick, but I'm not about to start letting him ruin my buzz, so I make a quick excuse from Dicko about wanting another pint and head over to him while he's getting his coins changed.

"Alright mate?" I say, not facing him like, just looking forward, waiting for the barman. He turns to me though.

"Yeah, you?"

"Yeah, buzzin' mate, been lookin' forward to this like."

"Me an'all," he says, and I have to say it's very unconvincingly.

"Good," I say, "don't take any notice of Dizzy yeah? He's just havin' a good time."

"Well tell him to stay out of my way then," he growls, like he's some sort of fuckin' hard man! Honestly. Some people, you give 'em an inch and they take a fucking mile. I can't say I didn't warn him. I shake my head, and turn to face him.

"Have it your way pal, but he'd knock the shit out of yer, that's all I'm sayin', have a good one yeah?" I say, leaving him to it. I'm fucked if I'm trying any more than I have, I'm here to make sure my boy Dicko has the best stag do ever, not babysit his sulking fucking brother-in-law. The cunt's still looking mumpy as fuck, and he won the fucking jackpot for fuck's sake! For sure, there's no pleasing some cunts. Fuck it, I tried and failed, the moral of the story, as Homer Simpson would say, is never try.

I head to the pisser, which is one of those strange blue affairs, where it seems like everything's white but they choose that mindfuck UV type blue lighting, that stuff that buzzes like fuck and you may as well be pissing in the dark 'cause you've got your eyes shut to keep out that harsh lighting. It's a small room, which houses a couple of urinals, a sink with a space where the mirror used to be, and, the reason for my being here, a single cubicle. The lock on the door's been smashed off by angry bouncers so many times that there's a huge chunk of wood with a dead bolt screwed in to it that serves as my only protection between my charlie and that twitchy cunt that was looking after the front door. The bog seat's been taken away to act as a deterrent from other folk like me partaking in the old snifter, but the back of the cistern looks perfectly good for it, so I've got a scrunched up bit of bog paper and I'm preparing my surface, before pulling out one of the many bags of class A drugs I've got in my wallet. I pull at the little grip seal on the bag, and gently tip it, squeezing it to open its sexy little mouth, and tapping its back. The coke falls into a pile on the porcelain surface, and with my card I shape it into a generous slug that's almost leaving slug territory and making a very welcome trip into *log* territory. For sure, it's almost as long as me, but that's how I like it, no point doing stuff by halves!

I stoop down over the albino slug with my rolled up purple queenie, and pull the coke up into my appreciative nostril and throat. I get that wave over me that I love, like I'm gonna faint, but it only lasts less than a second before I'm upright and letting the blood rush around my body, I feel a light prickle running through me, and I feel fucking brilliant. This promises to be a *very* good night!

The Pimp
Real Name: Lee 'Dicko' Dickinson
Age: 25
Occupation: Self Employed Plumber
Likes: His fiancée, Fiona & playing Fifa 2006
Dislikes: Smack heads & Politics
Most Likely to Dance to: The Clash - London Calling

"I love to eat lettuce for breakfast, they call me bunny," The Pimp has his hands tightly against Superman's cheeks, squashing them in together, then spreading them taut, the outer edges of his lips almost making a surprise meeting with his ears, "brilliant line that, that's how I pulled our Fiona." The Pimp releases The Man Of Steel's face and turns to his assembled crew, behind them Jesus returns from the toilet, his head nodding gratefully to the dubstep soundtrack. The Pimp holds his arms, and pint aloft, and salutes his best man, whose arms raise to match those of his friend.
"I love to eat lettuce for breakfast!" The Pimp hollers in the direction of the King of the Jews.
"They call me bunny!" Jesus provides the standard response, and like the seasoned professionals that they are, they open their gullets and fill them with the remains of their lager, which has a slight chemical

taste because they're too fresh after the lines being flushed, but whilever they have a percentage of alcohol in them they will do just as good a job as any other pint. The boys aren't in a state of mind where the taste of the drink is anything other than an aside, the sole function being to silently perform an almighty genocide of their respective brain cells. Superman's face is slightly contorted in confusion, it's almost as if he's not sure if he can smell a fart, but is hesitant to sniff up *just in case* that it is a fart that he is sensing and might fell his throat with the expelled gas of another man.

"Wait, I don't get it," says Superman, who beckons The Incredible Hulk over, "Joe, listen at this," he says, then turns to The Pimp, "say it again."

I love to eat lettuce for breakfast, they call me bunny," The Pimp repeats, this time directing his line to the green superhero. The Incredible Hulk stares off in wonderment as he processes the phrase, it's entered his ears, and is rattling around his brain, running along on a conveyor belt through several filters. It bypasses his logic filter completely as he already knows that, given that either Jesus of The Pimp has said it, it will make little or no logical sense. The phrase is almost ready to drop into the discarded joke bin, something slightly *too* obscure for his own brain, but then something clicks.

"Do you eat the lettuce straight from the lady garden?" he asks, holding his almost empty bottle in the way of The Pimp, whose face lights up.

"I do my good man, I do!" he laughs, over the moon that he's had his choice of chat-up line verified by an external source. He remembers meeting his wife-to-be, the woman of his dreams. He'd been in Kingdom nightclub with Jesus a couple of years ago one Saturday night, and they were amusing themselves with dares of approaching random women with even more random chat up lines that made little sense to anybody but the pair of them. The lines had been compiled the week earlier, where they'd got stoned at Jesus' and played on the Xbox for the night. They had a whole barrel of in-jokes between them, and this was no different. The pair were thick as thieves. On the night that he'd met his beloved future wife, they'd been spurned by many a girl, since they'd essentially just approached them and said a bizarre collection of words which made no sense. He'd spotted Fiona across the bar that seperated the pedestrian zone from the altogether more dangerous dance floor. She'd been wearing a multi-coloured dress which clung so nicely to her curves. She was standing across the way, hovering by the edge of the dancing area, arms folded and holding a bottle of a generic vodka based fruit drink, identified by seemingly unconnected letters, something like *HIV* or *STI,* and she was watching her friend, later to be identified as Shelley, her future maid of honour. The Pimp was smitten. She smiled away at her friend acting the clown around a fella, only interrupted by The Pimp, sidling up alongside her with a ridiculously big smile on his face.

"What you smilin' at?" she'd asked.

"You," he'd said, "you're gorgeous."

If she was put out by his interruption she'd never let on, just shook her head and thanked him, cool as hell. "I love to eat lettuce for breakfast," he'd shouted into her ear, but still never taking his eyes from hers, "they call me bunny!"

He'd watched her eyes widen as she absorbed his line, then turned to face him, cracking up with laughter and shaking her head.

"You daft cunt!" she'd roared, slapping his arm, throwing her head back to inhale deeply between her laughter, "and I'm guessing you're wanting to eat *my* lettuce tomorra mornin' eh?"

The Pimp had nodded with a smile, definitely feeling the come-on, "that alright?"

She'd shaken her head, no, slightly deflating his ego somewhat, but there was still a positive aura about her, and she wasn't gazing upon him with any kind of contempt.

"Got a fella?" he'd asked of her, this must surely have been the only reason that she'd not fall for his charms hook, line, and sinker, and the only barrier to him having her writhing beneath him in a sweaty heap. She shook her head.

"Nope."

"So, how comes you don't wanna come back to mine?"

She snorted with laughter again, but for some reason he didn't feel at all patronised, there was something about her that seemed eminently approachable that set him at ease. She'd stopped laughing again, but as she'd analysed the hope in his face she cracked out laughing again, through the hyperventilation and the tears she managed to stop enough to speak.

"You're serious? 'Cause I'm not yer common slag mate," she'd said, concreting her status as a woman he just *needed* to know. She'd got his chat-up line for a start, she'd actually *got it* as the exercise in daftness for which he and Tom were known, but the fact that she'd taken it totally in her stride and held her own without getting super embarrassed or taking offence. It marked her as a good sport, and that was almost as important to him as the fact that she was without a doubt the best looking girl in the building.

"My name's Lee," he'd said, holding out his hand for her to take, "what's yours?"

"Fiona."

"Can I get you a drink?"

"Nah, just got one, but you can get my number if you want?"

And the rest, as they say, was history. They'd gone on their dates, all five of them, before he'd finally plucked up the courage to as her if she'd wanted to stay over, which she did. She'd moved in by the end of the year, and they were engaged within six months. Since then, nothing has ever felt more right than his love for her, he feels like she completes him, and tonight he has every intention of getting extremely messy in her honour.

Beetlejuice
Real Name: Gavin 'Fingers' Fing
Age: 22
Occupation: Call Centre Operative
Likes: Winning when he's gambling & Prawn cocktail crisps
Dislikes: Losing when he's gambling & Women who treat him like shit
Most Likely to Dance to: Queen - We Will Rock You

They've moved on and Beetlejuice is beginning to feel the booze warming his bones, he's always been of the mind-set that if you get pissed easily then that's a good thing, it means you won't spend a lot of money. However, when you've been consuming beer at the rate that the boys have so far, then you're not going to last long, and Beetlejuice feels that he's going to fall way before the finish line. He doesn't take drugs like the others do, he's scared of them. At home he likes to smoke an occasional spliff but his poison will always be lager, he doesn't like the idea of chemicals destroying his body. He's seen some pictures of celebrities with decimated noses from cocaine abuse, he's seen the effects of heroin on others, the vilification that people get from their choice of drug. Beetlejuice doesn't want that. He doesn't think that any drug will ever be worth that, but he's among friends, good mates that he would never judge. They look out for him, will always look after him if he finds himself in trouble. He knows that the stick they give to him is borne of affection, not malice.

The group has already begun to dissipate into smaller, more manageable chunks of people, even though they're all moving together. Beetlejuice has found himself in on a round with Big Poppa Smurf and Bungle from Rainbow, and he's happy enough with that. At some point he'll have to buy a drink for The Pimp, but that's fine. It's the huge rounds that he's eager to avoid, ones where he's forced to buy drinks for other people that cost three times as much as his own, and then when they return the favour his drink costs a third as much as theirs did. He's secretly hoping that they forget that he's one of the only ones who are yet to get a round of Tequilas in. He hates spending money on anybody but himself. He won't give anything away unless it's somebody else's. That's just how he is and he comes under a load of fire for it. Beetlejuice checks his wallet and he's gutted to note that he's already spent half of his budget, admittedly some of that was on the taxi, but he didn't expect to be getting through the cash this quickly, and he's not sure that sixty quid is going to be enough. In the haze of his inebriation the memory of Al Capone dropping the bandit earlier sparks an impulsion. His hands dip deep into his striped black and white pockets, his fingers dredging through the change, feeling for the tell-tale rough edges of pound coins. He knows that he shouldn't, simply because the money he has isn't enough as it is, but he's got a good feeling about it. Al Capone won, and he was a nasty piece of work, so if a nice guy like Beetlejuice was to play the gambler, then surely lady luck would help him out? He hopes so, and approaches the machine tentatively. It greedily takes his coin, and allows him all of ten seconds of play before his cash is spent, and it's now blinking generally in his direction again, reminding him that it will happily take another in exchange for another crack of the whip. Another coin goes in, then another, then another. Before he knows it Beetlejuice has spent twelve quid, he has no more coins available to him but he has fifty quid in notes. The bandit hasn't even given him a sniff of action, but he's thinking that it might only take another few pounds for it to crank into life, and he'd be gutted if he witnessed somebody else win the money he'd put into it on a single go, especially if it was Al Capone, whose stare he can feel burning into his back. He *knows* that Capone will step right in as soon as he walks away. Capone is like a vulture, mentally circling him, waiting for him give up, and Beetlejuice can't have that. He needs change, but the second he goes to the bar he knows that Capone will jump into his grave, win the money that rightfully belongs to Beetlejuice, and then he'll claim innocence, say that he never saw the undead prankster at the bandit. He looks sadly and doubtfully at the orange note in his hands. His only hope of keeping the bandit at his mercy is sliding the note into the thin slot. The machine sucks the tenner from the air, but spits it right back out. Beetlejuice knows that this should be a sign that he should take his money and walk away, but he doesn't. He pulls the note, folds down the centre of it to try to get a degree of rigidity to it, and pushes it back into the slot. It slurps the paper again, and this time swallows it, converting five quid into playing funds immediately, much to his chagrin. He remembers when they took two quid and gave you the rest back, but now they've changed. It just *assumes* that he wants to spend a fiver. His mood descends into despondency as the fiver is depleted quicker than the pint that Jesus has just poured down his neck, and as the others cheer him Beetlejuice can't bring himself to join in, he's panicking now, wishing that he'd not even started this. He's already seventeen quid down and about to transfer another fiver into the playing fund, and he's literally only been playing for less than five minutes. It's starting to feel like it's not going to be his night, and it's not just the fact that he's killing his beer fund either. It's that he *always* does this, he's notorious for it. No matter how many times he does it he never learns. He's into his fifty pence's worth of goes on the bandit, and it drops two cherries in once, offering the chance to hold them which he does. His last go, before he'll be forced to change yet more money, and it offers him the chance to hold them again, and again he does. Between the cherries drops a lemon. Now, Beetlejuice knows how the bandits work. If he had an extra go it would either instruct him to hold them again, and it would guarantee him a go at the board, or it would just not offer the hold again, and he'll be back to square one. The drawback right now, is that he only has two twenty pound notes left. He really can't afford to change any more, or he'll be heading back to Sheffield on an early train. He's spent over twenty quid in less than the time it took him to drink a three quid pint, and now he's feeling slightly sick.

He's wishing he could go back in time, just a few moments, back to where he thought that this was a good idea. He pulls a purple note tight, his eyes drift from the Queen's face to the hungry slot. He can sense Al Capone edging ever closer to the machine, all that Beetlejuice needs is fifty fucking pence, and all that he has is forty fucking pounds. Without realising that he's doing it he's made the tell-tale crease through the middle of the note, and with all the finesse of an elderly Parkinson's patient playing *here comes the aeroplane* with a doting grandchild, he shakingly glides the money toward the bandit. Its crisp edge tickles at the lip of the flashing red mouth, and the whore of a gambler can sense the currency, it can almost *taste* it, but alas, the sensual foreplay between raging gambling addict and his bulky mistress is interrupted so rudely.

"Fingers! Your round for the shots mate!" Big Poppa Smurf calls to him. Gutted is not the word for Beetlejuice right now. He's over twenty quid down, and now he's going to be forced to spend another half of his budget on shots for the lads. He does have money in the bank, but it's already been earmarked for next month's rent, Beetlejuice cannot help but feel like he's fucked up royally. He offers the bandit a solemn parting glance, and resigns himself to the fact that this is not one bullet is going to be able to dodge. He's already been bought five shots, it's his duty to pay for a round. Trudging slowly away from the source of his own personal torment he pauses, winces at the sound of a selfish wanker slotting a pound coin in. Beetlejuice turns to see the back of Al Capone, clearly not uncomfortable with the unspoken law of ethics that says he should at least wait to see if the guy's finished. At the bar he orders ten shots of the cheapest house whiskey, he can physically *feel* himself holding on to the note as the girl behind the bar attempts to take it from his grasp, and feels the world fade away from him as the raw tasting alcohol burns his throat and stomach. Behind the burn, and the water in his eyes, he feels real tears ball up as Capone wins yet another jackpot. *His* jackpot.

***

He's a tight cunt that Fingers. Honestly, spends all his cash ont bandits then complains when he's skint. It's not like it's even *that* enjoyable, I mean, think about it. You spend pound after pound after fucking pound on pressing a button, which not-so-randomly selects a combination of fruits and numbers which may, or may not decide to throw you a few crumbs as recompense for the wages you're wasting on the pleasure. Nah, fuck that. For sure, if I'm gonna blow thirty quid it's gonna be on a few hours of party powder, and I'm probably gonna blow it five or six times over in a night, but you know what? It's *my* fucking money, I'll spend it on whatever the fuck I want to. So now I'm seeing the hypocritical nature of that last statement, like, I've bitched about that poor cunt then gone and said that I can do what I want with my money, but ask me if I give a fuck. Go on, seriously, ask me. The answer to your question, dear reader, is nope, not one fucking bit. Fingers has got his vice and I've got my many vices. But, the thing is, do I mope about after I've made my investment in a good time the way that he's moping about just now? I won't tell you to ask me if I mope, you can tell me from my happy, hazy and very fucking chipper demeanour that moping just isn't my thing. Mope. Moping. Mope. Good word. I like it, say it out loud. Brilliant word. Mope. Anyway, I'm sidetracked by hilarious-to-say-if-you-really-think-about-it words, my point is, what fun is there in a vice that turns your face into the proverbial slapped arse? Unless you're coming down, of course, but I'm sure there'll be time in the story for that later, let me just enjoy myself first for fuck's sake, don't start pecking my head about what's to come.

Anyway, Fingers puts his shot glass down on the bar, and he's in danger of killing my mood with his droopy morose face, like, I can see why he's mostly upset, and it's that the big cunt Tony has just dropped yet another jackpot from a gambler, and that jackpot is predominantly consisting of money that our boy Fingers has pumped into it. The daft cunt. My gaze shifts from Tony back to Fingers who's looking right at me, and this kid's in danger of bursting into tears. *No mate, grow the fuck up.* I make my excuses from Dicko and weave through the lads to get to the dumpy gambling prick. His costume's actually not bad at all, aside from him being a bit shorter than Michael Keaton was in the actual film, quite a bit shorter too. He got the suit from Dazzler's Fancy Dress, and his mum to sort the make-up out. She's done a good job old Mrs F, she's a good bird, fuck knows how she puts up with our Fingers on her own, I'm not sure he'll ever move out, even if there's ever a time that he could afford it.

"Alright mate? What's up wi' your face?" I ask as I approach him, he's not looking at me though, he's chucking some right daggers at Tony, honestly, if looks could kill then that cunt would be twitching on the floor, begging the Almighty Whoever to offer mercy and allow him the opportunity to breathe again, but then that imaginary deity would see the shitty look that Fingers is shooting and to be honest, with them daggers, for sure I think that deity would shit it. *You're on your own pal!* He, or she, or *it* would say.

"Fucked up ant I?" he's saying, of course he has, he always fucking does.

"Why? What's up pal?"

"Fuckin', blown twenty quid on the gambler, and now *that cunt,* has fuckin' won it, first press an'all," he moans, shaking his head, "can't fuckin' believe it. Only got twenty quid left now after that round."

I really hope he's not expecting sympathy here. Okay, for one, it's a stag do, who the fuck goes out with less than a couple of hundred? For two, it was his choice to play the stupid thing. But he's a mate, and I'm struggling to maintain my frustration with the silly get.

"What you playin' 'em for if you're skint silly bollocks? Eh?" I've gone for the half-frustrated, half-concerned approach, that kind of big brother-little brother way. Not that I have any brothers, but I've seen enough films to know the tone. Fingers shakes his head again.

"Dunno, thought I could win some beer tokens, fucked up though, and *that cunt,* he fuckin' saw me mate, he actually watched me and then jumped straight in. Lucky twat."

I'm not about to start causing more trouble with Tony over it, 'cause the way I see it is he won that money fair and square. I mean, yeah, he didn't have to do it so blatantly and under the nose of poor Fingers, but what was he supposed to do? I've no intention of being the shithead who just keeps rocking up and threatening him for other people, it's not my style, besides, I've got my own shit to worry about, such as the hankering I've got to throw some more chee-chee up my snout, and now that I'm think about *that,* my mood is swinging a little bit round to annoyed again. I hope I'm not gonna be babysitting and moderating all through Dicko's wedding an'all, 'cause I did *not* sign up for that shit as best man. I decide to just play it straight down the line with Fingers.

"Look, you win some you lose some, if yer not prepared to lose then don't fuckin' play 'em," I say, but that hangdog, pathetic look on his face, it just -----
----

--Gimme it back later, you daft--

-------------------------------Nobody around, I can----------

----

---------------------- hammering on the cubicle door, and
he's shouting my name.

"Come on Tommy, you finished wipin' yer arse yet pal?"

"No, it's like am melting from inside out mate, fuck off and leave me to it! Could be wipin' for weeks!" I shout back to him. He's a great lad Dicko, honestly, never met a lad who can match me for banter like him.

"Make sure you stop wipin' when there's blood kidda, you don't want bits of shit floating round yer system," and I'm thinking, *You're already fulla shit,* and *You're enough of a shithead as it is,* I can see it coming, "'cause you're fulla shit as it is!"

Boom! Coulda won myself a fiver. I don't know whether it's because he's predictable as fuck or if we're both just flying the same flag, but fuck it. It was funny. I flush the toilet to mask the sound of me unrolling my coke-snorting note, and putting the quickly diminishing gram back with the others, before I open the cubicle to see the expectant, and impatient faces of three of my very best mates, each of them waiting for their go in the cubicle. I pass Dicko who's already edging his way in through the door and we touch knuckles, honestly, I fuckin' love that bloke.

The lads have pretty much drunk up when I return to the main bar, all ready to go, just waiting on our boys in the bogs. Fingers comes up to me smiling, fuck knows why, he's skint as fuck.

"Cheers again for that Tom, I'll get it back to you when we pass a bank."

I'm wondering what the fuck he's on about, but I'm sure it'll come out in the wash.

Big Poppa Smurf
Real Name: Justin 'Justin' Heaton
Age: 24
Occupation: Part time barman/ Part time drug dealer
Likes: Cocaine & breasts
Dislikes: Jobsworth cunts & Nosy neighbours
Most Likely to Dance to: The Prodigy - No Good (Start the Dance)

"Dizzy! Wait up! I need to get some cash out!" Big Poppa Smurf called to Hitler. The nazi leader spun-wobbled on his heels to face the bearded blue cartoon character, offered a Hitler Salute, and sparked up a cigarette, gazing around Millennium Square, watching the rest of the gang head up the stairs to the Wetherspoons. A pair of girls, or women, rounded the corner as Big Poppa Smurf caught up with his mate, and grabbed his attention.

"Ladies!" he bellowed. The eldest of the two appeared to be also the more responsive of the two, apparently she was aware of the Smurfs, and was a big fan. From the rapidly diminishing distance between them, as she tottered toward him, arms flailing, eager to get her hands in his huge white beard, he could see her to be reasonably attractive, in that she-scrubs-up-well sense of the term. Her dirty blonde hair, complete with intentionally tousled extensions flapped in the evening breeze behind her, and the bra-less tits bounced very nicely, Big Poppa Smurf was happy to note, in the rose pink tight dress she was sporting. The dress itself rode up to reveal a fake-tanned and smooth pair of quality pins. Although her face was also a thing of beauty his eyes couldn't drag themselves away from the top of her thighs, if she just tottered a few feet more then Big Poppa Smurf would have front row tickets to the panty show. Unfortunately for the king of the mythical creatures she'd reached him literally inches from where that could have been a possibility, her hands curling in and around the synthetic dirty white beard, pulling it from his face only to twang the thing back against it, sending curly spirals right up his nose and into his mouth.

"Eyup Mr Smurf!" she spoke in her deep but nasal West Yorkshire way, her voice betraying her beauty by coming out somewhere between Scary Spice and Keith Lemon. He wasn't going to allow it to put him off though, the offence his ears had taken would be brushed completely and unashamedly under the carpet owing to the pleasure that his eyes were taking.

"Now then ladies," he said, his pure white eyes peeping out and smiling from the blue, his right hand sliding on to the Leeds girl's waist, his little finger toying with the idea of sliding further round and on to her backside. She took it in her stride and pushed closer to his chest as he purred, "aren't you gorgeous?"

"Thanks, not so bad yerself mate."

"You girls going Wetherspoons?"

"Yeah you?"

"We certainly are, come wi' me, I'll get you a drink."

The exchange was short, but sweet, and Big Poppa Smurf held his crooked arm for the latest object of his desire to hook herself on to. As they walked he could hear Hitler speaking to the girl's sidekick, his voice filled with stunned wonder.

"It might be the drugs, but, honestly, you're honestly, the most beautiful woman I have ever seen. Honestly."

"Honestly?" the girl deadpanned, trudging alongside Hitler since her pal had binned her off.

Through his laughter Big Poppa Smurf felt moved to ask his new companion.

"So what's yer name then gorgeous?"

"Sasha, what's yours?"

"Big Poppa Smurf, but you can call me Justin," he said as they approached the steps up to the front door of the pub, and entered the place. The lads were already served and in the corner, visible through the mass of cig smoke. It wouldn't be long before the smoking ban came into force, especially since the Scottish had theirs recently. Big Poppa Smurf was indifferent. Some of his mates, and his dad's mates had bitched about it, but the reality of the situation was that if they banned it then they banned it, you could complain 'til the cows came home, but you'd just be complaining in the rain come this time next year.

"Pint of lager an' a rum an' coke please pal," he asked of the barman, who turned to grab a tumbler and pushed it up against the three pronged measured optic, a second thought hit him and he turned to Hitler, "what you havin' pal?"

"Same as you mate, want owt?" Hitler asked of his own companion, who shook her head, an independent girl it seemed, who was prepared to buy her own drink, or fearful or having it spiked if she had no control over it. Big Poppa Smurf didn't actually care enough to consider it further than that, but added the drink to his order and the four of them skirted through the crowd toward the rest. Al Capone, once again, was away at the bandit, an Embassy fag dangling from his lips, the ash dropping periodically onto the buttons before him. Pockets of the gang had noted the presence of ladies, and had begun to worm their way over. Big Poppa Smurf had done the ground work, and had even paid for a drink, so he was in no way going to allow any of the rest of them to weasel in so easily. As far as he was concerned her unnamed mate was fair game though, so good luck to them. If he had to put his money on any of them to work their magic, then the smart money was on Jesus, the miraculous bastard.

Bungle
Real Name: Andrew 'Jackson' Jackson
Age: 25
Occupation: Session musician/Busker
Likes: Playing gigs & Controlling the CD player at any get together
Dislikes: Any performer made famous by television talent shows & Buffet food
Most Likely to Dance to: Led Zeppelin - Whole Lotta Love

He's in the toilet cubicle of the Wetherspoons, pulling at the zip on the inside of his suit, cursing the day that he ever thought it would be a good idea to wear it, instead of a less cumbersome paint based outfit, like Big Poppa Smurf. The only outfit worse, he now considers, would be a Harold Shipman suit and beard wheeling a barrow full of elderly corpses, but even then at least he wouldn't be sweating cobs from every pore. The coke and pills aren't helping his perspiration any, and Bungle is beginning to feel slightly wheezy. For every hot, sticky breath he takes, the filter at the front does a very good job of throwing that breath right back into his face. A cold bead of sweat tickles through the hairs at the base of his spine and enters his already sopping, and sore, arse crack. Through the fug of his inebriation and the increasing sweatiness his fingers pick ever more clumsily against the inside of the outfit, without success. He's not panicking, nor is he irritated, the MDMA simply will not allow that. He'll simply try another avenue of tactic.

Bungle reconsiders his situation. He's struggling to remove his human form from the exterior of the hatted bear man, and all he wants to do is get another line of cocaine into his human nose. He isn't naked in there, he was warned by the proprietor of Dazzles to never even consider going commando, so his hands worm themselves out of those of the costume, and wander south to his interior pockets, feeling for that tell-tale feel of the leather of his wallet. There's a part of him that wonders why he never thought of this to begin with. His costume is basically a walking shield from prying eyes. His fingers pick at the edge of the wallet, pulling it open and wriggling around the concealer pocket until they place themselves over the ridge of the grip seal on his bag of coke, and edge the thing further into his grasp. With his other hand he digs around for his house keys, shaking each pocket hoping for that dull jangle. From the outside, in the toilet cubicle, Bungle resembles a zombied comedy bear man whose insides are being attacked beneath the skin, by thick tentacles, or worms, which are eating away at him, bulging out his fur, then disappearing to feast on his cotton wool guts. On the inside however, those wormlike creatures are his arms, attempting an ambitious endeavour, which is to open the bag, dip into it with his key to scoop up a generous portion of the delicious white party powder, and then suck it deep into his face, and all in the confines of a not-so-loose Bungle costume. In the dark. He overcomes his first hurdle, and now has the tools of his work in the correct hands, the drugs in his left hand, the key in his right. The left hand remains pressed firmly between the rough fabric and the dripping wet shirt that sticks to his skin, and the right hand brings the key delicately up, once again soaked wet by his sweaty torso. The creature inside Bungle is overjoyed as this exercise appears to be a complete success, he holds his breath so that he will not exhale too sharply and dislodge the drugs, and with all the delicacy of a Japanese Fugu chef he brings his precious mound of cocaine further to his-

A heavy, and rapid series of thumps echo through his small cubicle and the creature inside Bungle jumps with a start. His key is empty.

"The fuck you doin'?" he calls out, unable to control the rage in his voice, this effort has been far too painstaking, and has been jeopardised by a pisshead with a serious urge to shit, "there's somebody in here for fucks sake!"

There's no verbal response from the outside of the cubicle. The creature inside Bungle struggles to regain his view from through the black filter which acts as both a window to the world, and his air ventilation unit. His breathing is heavy now, from the effort of holding it, and from the rapidly rising adrenalin. Whoever it is out there has ruined his moment, and seem intent on spoiling it further as they hammer once again on the cubicle door.

"Fuck off!" roars Bungle. He was never this angry when he was the mellow sidekick for the purposes of entertaining the children of the eighties and nineties, Bungle had never instructed Rod, Jane or Freddy to go fuck themselves with as much venom as he has displayed tonight. Even despite the great feeling that the MDMA is providing to him, Bungle is a man bear on the edge.

***

"So, Cassie, what do you do?" I'm asking this very attractive little chicky that Justin's fetched into the pub with him. She's got a proper, not-fake-at-all tan, and it looks natural like, maybe one of her parents is Italian or something. She's got these really good eyes, like, they're massive, there's loads of white to go with the sparkling brown beads in the middle of them. For sure, I can't stop looking right at her, like, right into those eyes, I'm finding myself getting lost in them, and to be honest, I'm enjoying it. I'm getting so lost in them that I'd need a fucking map and a compass to get back out. At this exact moment, I think I love her. I want to tell her how beautiful she is, it's not exactly a sexual thing, it's just that, well------------------------------
----

----------------------------How the fuck did I pull you?
Really? For sure, you're--

--Dizzy's pulling at my
arm, and I can't make out what he's saying, I'm not
sure I care just now, I only want to return my lips to
hers, feel my face melt into hers again. His words
begin to make sense beneath the noise of the other
punters in the pub, and this increasing sound of men
shouting, women screaming, bottles, glasses and
tables being thrown to the floor. Cassie's already
huge eyes widen even further, something is defo
happening behind me, and the fact that Justin and

Dicko are scarpering across the floor toward the ruckus tells me that it's one of our lot that's in trouble. I plant a smacker on Cassie's lips and turn to see what's happening. There's two bouncers holding on to this giant fuzzy turd monster by the legs, and there's another two up at the head end. The fuzzy turd monster is writhing, and it's funny but it kinda looks like they're a really shitty pissed up Chinese dragon thing, you know like where they have all the people underneath the actual dragon thing? Well yeah, that's what it looks like, but as the fuzzy turd monster wriggles loose from the blokes holding its legs I see that it's only fucking Jackson, complete with his Bungle outfit. Without thinking I'm straight over there to get my boy's back, but there's two more bouncers warning us off as the others try to drag our lad Jackson out. Fuck knows what he's done, he's generally a placid kid so I'm sure he's not started a fight, *then* you chuck into the mix the fact that he's flying on those pills he's had, I don't get it.

"What's he done?" I'm half shouting-half asking the fat fucker that's warning us off, but he's still concentrating on backing every cunt off. You know that he's itching to collar some cunt an'all, like, anyone that gets pulled into the centre of gravity will get ejected from the pub an'all, so I'm still asking, and he's still ignoring. Dicko's pushing against the bouncer on the other side and Justin's up at the front-

----

--Gav get onto the police, these cunts are trouble------------------------
----

----------------------Jackson's standing there, his
costume ripped as fuck, pointing like a mad man at
the bouncer who's looks like he's in charge of
proceedings here, Dicko and Fingers are trying to
placate him, but he's not helping my trying to calm
the situation down. The girls have come with us,
which was nice of them.

"You don't need to get bobbies mate, we'll sort him
out," I'm reasoning with the bloke but he's standing
there like an erect cock, his stony face grinding down
on to this chewing gum like it's just fucked his mum
and he's come downstairs to find it using his
favourite mug, and he's refusing to make eye contact.
He's defo not playing the game, "what you bein' a
cunt for?"

This does it. His beady little eyes dart my way, and
he's bristling a little bit. Jackson's still shouting the
odds from behind us. The walking erection stops
chewing.

"Coppers are on their way, stick around and wait for
'em if yer want, or you can take your mate, and fuck
off."

His head nods back behind us, and his arm comes up
all slow like, and with two fingers of his hand he
flicks them, as if to *shoo* me away. Any other time, if
he'd dissed me like that I'd be inclined to knock the
shitbag on his arse, I'm not soft you know, but I've got
about five gram of coke on me, and a gram of MDMA,
I can't be losing that. For sure, if we got nabbed by
the bobbies, my first and only regret would be the

drugs I lost. I look at the bloke and shake my head through sheer disappointment.

"You fuckin' prick," I whisper with an inane wannabe psycho grin on my chops, and turn to face the rest of them, "come on lads, this is wank."

Al Capone
Real Name: Tony Grimbleby
Occupation: Banker
Age: 32
Likes: Making money & Submissive women
Dislikes: Lending money out & The derisive laughter of women
Most Likely to Dance to: Coldplay – Yellow

"Boys, they've got coppers on the way so we're gonna have to split up for a bit," Jesus says, looking at the historically inaccurate retro Casio watch on his wrist, his face clumsily gurning as he addresses the assembled team, "it's only ten, taxi's not 'til three, shall we call it an hour and then get down to Majestyk's?"

Several heads nod in agreement, other faces look to around for affirmation. They begin to edge together as the realisation dawns on them that if they're splitting up then they'll want to be grouped with their better mates, much as it was in school when the teacher would declare that the forthcoming exercise would require that they be in teams. Friends would eyeball each other across the classroom, unspoken pacts that they would seek each other out come the judgment day. The only pitfall would be others beating you to the punch and you found yourself in a group with the kid with the thick glasses who smelled like damp, and the girl with the calliper, under the heading *Miscellaneous.* Right now Al Capone is eyeballing nobody, he doesn't really know any of them. He can see Superman edging ever closer to The Incredible Hulk, seemingly immortal blokes together, the pair of them have also got Hitler shuffling toward them. Across from them it looks like Jesus, The Pimp, and Big Poppa Smurf have got big plans on disappearing together, along with the two girls they've managed to acquire. Al Capone is on edge right now, because it looks like he's going to get tagged in with Beetlejuice, a dishevelled looking half Bungle/half Jackson, dripping with sweat and starting to shiver in the night air, and King Smurf, who are looking like the *miscellaneous* crew. Now, Al Capone is *not* happy about being placed with this gang, because for one, Bungle Jackson is the one who's put them in this situation, and if the coppers are looking for anybody then it's him. For another, the only one he actually knows here is his future brother-in-law, The Pimp.

"I'm comin' wi' you," he says to The Pimp, his tone says that there's no two ways about this. The Pimp looks briefly to the King of the Jews, it's only a flicker, but it's long enough for Al Capone to register it. He knows he wasn't wanted here tonight, but he's thick skinned enough to let his slide, and ride the piece of shit night out. There's one last reason that he's not leaving The Pimp's side, and that's that his two cronies, Jesus and Big Poppa Smurf, are notorious lady's men, and given that there are two women in tow, he cannot trust The Pimp to keep his slimy cock in his pants, he will *not* allow the dirty cunt to break his sister's heart.

"No worries pal," Jesus says, nodding away, a dozy smile dripping from his head, combined with that same gurning which is starting to get on Al's tits. Jesus snakes a sleazy arm around the shoulder of the younger of the girls, the one whose face he'd been eating off before it all kicked off in the pub, and he's whispered something in her ear. She looks at Al Capone and laughs, before turning and whispering a response. Al feels a flush of blood to his face, and the hairs on the back of his neck stand up. He suddenly feels very alone and self-conscious. Big Poppa Smurf is clawing at the arse of her mate, and The Pimp is now looking at everybody.

"What we fuckin' waitin' for then? Majestyk's in an hour then yeah?"

The gang begin to head begrudgingly in their separate ways, mumbling about where they're going and Beetlejuice is apparently annoying Bungle Jackson with his attempts at banter about the last ten minutes' events, the last thing Al Capone sees as they turn the corner is Bungle thump Beetlejuice in his arm, and playfully pull his white undead head under his own arm, squeezing and dragging the born victim along with him. Al Capone watches the other crew disappear in the opposite direction, then turns to the newly depleted squad of Jesus, The Pimp, Big Poppa Smurf, and the two girls.

"What now?" he says, and aside from the set to that he'd previously had with Hitler, these are only the second words he's spoken to anybody all night, and it shows in the surprised face of Jesus.

"Me H. Christ!" he declares, "the boy speaks!"

Al Capone is more than irritated when the others break out in laughter, especially the girls who know him even less than everybody else. Capone feels that there is no laughter more derisive than that of girls. It cuts deep. He wants to grab the pair of them by the throats, crush them, squeeze every insulting bit of life from their skinny bodies, to ensure that they will never breathe again. Especially the one with Big

Poppa Smurf, her whiny nasal Leeds accent grates more than most. The air instantly turns frosty. The Pimp picks up on it first, and his smiling laughter stops. He knows that Al Capone is capable of throwing the dummy out of his cot, and is notorious for spoiling the most happy of celebrations. Alas, it's too late, Capone has clammed himself shut, his hands play with the ever growing pocket of pound coins, and he's about to blow.

"You know what? I din't even wanna fuckin' come tonight, only come 'cause of our Fiona fuckin' chelpin' at me. Youse are all fuckin' kids man, and you slags," he directs to the girls, who are instantly, and simultaneously affronted by the tag, Big Poppa Smurf tenses, an arm instinctively wraps around the shoulder of the one named Sasha, "go fuck yourselves yeah?"

Al Capone displays none of the coolness associated with his namesake, and flounces away in the opposite direction to everybody else, the departed gangs included. Aside from the sniggering he has induced in the girls, the only sounds at this minute are the heavy thuds of a bass line emanating from a pub or club somewhere around the Millennium Square, and the jangle of the pound coins in his heavy pocket. He has no idea where he is going to go, all he knows is that he really needs to get away from those people, because he would do something that he may end up regretting tomorrow. He hates his sister for putting him in this position. He hates her future husband for siding with the rest of the pricks. But most of all he hates the snidey, piss-taking bitches that have attached themselves to the posse. They don't know him, but they feel like they can take the piss as if they were best mates. Capone mutters profanities under his breath as he stomps heavily through the city, the slap of his white wing-tip shoes against the hard concrete is punctuated by the jangle of coins. He wishes that he could have got them changed before Bungle performed his almighty and selfish act of getting himself kicked out of the Wetherspoons, taking the rest of them with him. *Slap jingle slap jingle slap jingle-*

"'Scuse me pal," a voice calls from behind him, he turns to see a youth, appearing to be no more than about eighteen. He carries with him a yellow plastic bag, emblazoned with the *Netto* dog. Al Capone believes that the youth's worldly possessions are probably contained within the bag. He knows what's coming, and refuses to stop for the urchin, all he wants is to find the train station and get out of this fucking city.

"No thanks," Al Capone calls over his shoulder, but the kid is quick. He's up by his side in seconds, and effortlessly keeps pace with the drunken Capone.

"I don't want yer money," says the kid, a smile in his eyes, "just wondered if you had a spare fag I could buy?"

"Don't smoke," says Capone, still he marches on, refusing to make eye contact with the kid. He can feel his blood boiling, he wants this homeless bum to leave him alone.

"Okay, but is there any need to be such a dick?" Capone draws to a halt, and turns to the kid, grabs the front of his grease stained jacket, and hisses right into his face.

"Listen, you cheeky cunt-"

Capone is halted as the kid pulls closer to him, a sharp pain digs into his gut, and the kid is still smiling as he stares deep into his eyes. Capone looks to his belly, and the hypodermic syringe standing to attention from his shirt, the needle buried deep into his body, then back to the kid. He feels his head being tugged and twisted firmly round so that the kid can speak directly into his ear.

"Welcome to the AIDS club, you cheeky cunt."

Superman
Real Name: James 'Jimmy' Vickers
Age: 25
Occupation: Roofer
Likes: Catching sight of the woman who lives across from him undressing in her bedroom & The smell of tar
Dislikes: Public transport & The smell of farms
Most Likely to Dance to: The Shamen - Ebeneezer Goode

"That were mad as fuck, you see Jackson's face? Like a new born babby roarin' away! Drippin' he were! Fuckin' brilliant."

"Yeah, fuckin' nuts."

"So where we off?"

"I dunno, just keep walking eh?"

Superman is in high spirits, despite the last half an hour's events. He and the other two that he's been bundled with are bouncing along the street, already unintentionally misremembering the story. By tomorrow Superman will have sliced at least three bouncers in half with his laser beam eyes, Bungle will have feasted upon their charred remains with indiscriminate rage, The Incredible Hulk will have smashed the place to pieces with his angry fists, and Hitler, well, everybody knows what he's capable of. The trio negotiate Boar Lane, looking for an establishment that will match their happy mood. They pass McDonalds, and Superman catches the attention of a gathering of females waiting to fill their gorgeous faces with meat. Superman sniggers at the innuendo laden thought of filling each and every one of their faces with meat, and is given an idea. Superman bounds heroically to the side entrance door, almost ripping it from its hinges as he jumps into the establishment, grabbing a handful of his own cock.

"Eeyarr girls! You can fill yer faces wi' this meat for free!" he bellows into the fast food restaurant. There are some couples in the place who shake their heads at the childish behaviour of the protector of humankind, but the majority of the drunks in there find it as hilarious as he does. The girls whose attention he had caught cheer in unison, a particularly chubby one tramps over, flesh spills out from between where the skirt fails to meet the too-tight bright purple matching top. It gloops out but hangs precariously, as if it were the teenage snot filled phlegm of a kid holding his spit above the ground using only his own lips and the spit's viscosity, before he sucks it right back up and into his mouth. She approaches and takes her own handful of his member, her fingers doing their best to tickle at his nuts, before she slides her cigarette tasting tongue into his mouth, her hand still working at his cock. Unfortunately for the delightful girl, Superman is high as a kite on MDMA, and has no strong sexual feelings right now, but he is loving the sensation of her fleshy hip in his hand. To him it reminds him of a slightly softer version of the stress ball on the desk in the office at work. The kiss seems to last forever. Hitler and The Incredible Hulk hammer on one side of the window, and the girl's friends give it the *whoooooo!* as they stomp their feet and cheer the brief lovers, before his new best friend pulls away and he gazes at her in wonderment.

"You are gorgeous," he says, his eyes saucer-wide. The girl smiles, and her right hand slithers down over her breasts, and her gut, snaking into the front of the dress, and into the gusset of her knickers. Still she holds on to Superman's cock with the other hand which shows absolutely no sign of life. The right hand comes back out from inside her knickers, and with a filthy look in her eyes she wipes her glistening fingers across the whole of his top lip. On any other day the smell that rises into his nostrils might give Superman's gag reflex a bit of stern exercise, it's got an aroma that resembles his slippers at home, a sweaty, cheesy, used kind of smell, it's the kind of smell that you could taste. But drunk, and smitten by this girl in McDonalds whose pungent fanny juice is smeared across his face, Superman could happily smell it forever. Alas, the boys want him back.

"Come on yer daft bastard!" Hitler calls from the door, to a *Heil Hitler!* response from the gang of girls. Instinctively his arm shoots forward and he obliges the pissheads with the salute, but his eyes remain on Superman, Hitler wants to drink, and dance, enjoy his night and the effects of the drugs in his blood, not watch his friend get fanny batter smeared over his face by what could quite easily be The Incredible Hulk's sister. Hulk stands back, laughing at the spectacle. He's never really been the most talkative of guys, never wants to be the centre of attention, but he really loves nothing more than watching those of his mates that do.

"Mate, she were gorgeous," says Superman as the trio continue along Boar Lane on their quest for a suitable venue for their next drink, Hulk looks doubtfully at his fellow superhero.

"Are yer eyes painted on?" he laughs, Superman's features take on a slightly hurt look, but Hulk is inclined to continue, "I wunta touched her wi' a stolen cock."

Hitler slaps a heavy hand against Superman's back and laughs loudly, the man of steel relents eventually, and joins in with the mirth as his tongue rolls across his top lip for the third time to take whatever remains of his lost love's lady juice. He's laughing, but secretly he's hoping he'll see her again.

***

"Campag Velocet?!" I'm shouting into the ear of the DJ who's leaning over the side of the booth, like a white, slightly melty Curly Wurly, he's that long, thin and seemingly bendy. Maybe it's just that the booth is raised up a bit but the walls of it are small, maybe it's just the drugs. Who the fuck knows? Anyway, he's leaning right over and he's nodding his head, you fucking beauty, I give him the thumbs up, my face must resemble that of a windowlicker with a brand new pack of crayons.

This pub is mental. The Dry Dock, I love it. I didn't believe it when I saw it from the outside, I mean, it's like, an *actual boat.* Cassie and Sasha brought us up here 'cause we're saying we want some decent quality music instead on all that dancey trancey shite, and already the White Curly Wurly has made me a very happy fucker. I'm bouncing back to the others to the soundtrack of Ian Brown telling me that dolphins were monkeys, and I'm in my element here. Dicko's nodding away, his hands drumming the table at the same time, likes to think he's a drummer. For sure, he's got rhythm, no doubt about that, but all he's doing is giving it the quick tempo hi-hat with his right hand, and the left hand's on snare duty. He's keeping the time pretty well, but if you stuck him behind an

actual drum kit he'd be a noisy octopus, smashing away on any and everything in front of him. Justin's sitting on a chair with his back to the wall and the girl Sasha's on his lap, acrossways like, her arms wrapped right around his neck, his hands are doing a good job of keeping her tits warm and they're forming this weird, slithering two bodied creature, attached at the face. There's a bouncer with his eye on them for in case it gets any more of a show, like, if his hands decide that they want to explore what lies beneath and all that. Got kicked out of a pub myself for that, when I were younger like, for sure, this girl was fair playing a good tune on the old spunk trumpet, nearly bit my cock off when the bouncer dragged up her off of her knees. Learned my lesson that day, now I'll always get my blow jobs up the back of a club, or in a bush or summat--
----

----------------I love this place, fuckin' mental-------------
----

---------*Say it louder, we drive the car faster. It's a tiki, disaster. See my tambourine, ain't no funki tangerine-* Yes! Right tune! I hoped he'd pick this one when I requested Campag Velocet. I'm back on my feet, dragging Cassie by the hand to the small dance floor, I'm going absolutely mental. The filthy sounds of Pete Voss talking seemingly pointless but at the same time evocative as fuck words at me over Lascelles Lascelle's ridiculously infectious drum beat are right up my street, he could give us the shipping forecast

and it'd still sound cool as fuck, me and Cassie are doing the pogo like absolute nobheads. He could tell me I was about to die and I'd still want to dance. For sure, she nearly bit my hand off when I offered her a bomb of MDMA, and now she's coming up it's fucking brilliant. I know for a fact that she's never heard of Campag, I don't know many that have to be fair, but when that dirty bass buzzes through your feet, and Pete's talking his stuff, you can't help but tap your feet, so when you're proper up, and I mean up up, you're gonna dance. Cassie's got a hold of my hand and we're not giving a fuck who we're bumping into, it's just me and Cass, Cass with the delicious ass, in this fucked up bubble. Fuck knows what everybody else is up to, fuck Jackson and his Bungle-based-bust-ups, fuck Tony and his chucking the dummy out, and most of all fuck this job I'm supposed to start on Monday. This is brilliant------------------------------------
----

--*I will bang it,
in your face!*---

------------------------You wanna come back to ours?-----

----------------------------*everybody's got some love inside
of 'em, everybody's got some love inside*------------------

--"Where we
going?" I'm saying, fuck knows where we are, this is

not the proper centre of Leeds any more. Cassie's dragging me along by the hand, chatting ten to the dozen now about this party at the big student house she lives at that we're off to in Hyde Park, she says she's told me four times but I'm fucked if I remember. Sasha and Justin are hanging back, he's got her up against a tree, snogging the fuck out of her face and Dicko's up with us, and he's telling me to remember we're supposed to be back at Majestyk's by now. For sure, Majestyk's is the least of my worries, I'm looking at my watch and it's coming up to midnight, we've still got three hours before the taxi comes, and I wanna go see what this party's all about. Justin and the girl Sasha catch us up and by now the pair of them have faces as blue as each other, they look a right pair. Funny.

"Remember we've got to be back in town for three, Fiona'll kill me if I don't get in that taxi," says Dicko, and I know he loves the girl, but he's not half scared of her.

"Does she knock you about Dicko?" I laugh, and he's shaking his head with a smile, "does she love you just slightly *too* much?"

"Yeah, I'll have fell down t'stairs and straight into a cupboard door by tomorra," he chuckles, but I know he's still shitting it, she don't half give him earache at times, but like I say, he loves her so it's his choice to be pussywhipped, I know the boy, if it ever got too much he'd be out of there like shit off a stick.

Beetlejuice

He looked at his watch, noting the time at about midnight. Surely everybody should have been here by now? King Smurf and Jackson had gone off in their own directions, and knowing Jackson as he did, the chances were that he'd spend most of his night in the bogs, clearly never one to learn his lesson from the Wetherspoons debacle. The Bungle outfit had been discarded before they'd even gone into the pub before here, doormen all over the city would undoubtedly on the lookout for the half man, half iconic bear that had wreaked havoc in one of its multitude of bars. Beetlejuice was well aware of how they were generally in touch with each other if there was a troublemaker on the loose, given that he'd taken a shoeing at the hands, or indeed feet, of some bouncers in Sheffield. The story was that he'd bumped into a girl in a club when he was out with Tom and some of the others, she was wearing the shortest skirt he had ever seen, her cheeks were basically hanging out from the bottom of it, and his hand had literally brushed past her backside, but she'd taken exception, started shouting to anybody that would listen that he'd tried to slip his fingers up her arse. She'd gone straight over to the bouncers who'd never bothered to listen to his stories of innocence, just took her at her word and dragged him from the premises. He'd ranted on the front door for a further five minutes but eventually they'd lost patience with him, and what seemed to be the head doorman took him to one side, and growled a threat which was violent enough to put the shits up him, so he'd accepted defeat and gone on to drink elsewhere, albeit alone. Every place he went to they had their eyes on him, and had set him on edge. The more he'd drunk the less stable he'd become, and by the end he was all over the place, he'd stumbled over the wrong man's table, and knocked over the wrong man's girlfriend's drinks, subsequently, both the wrong man and the bouncers broke his cheek bone, two of his ribs, and knocked out four of his teeth. In the busy foyer of the nightclub he licked the smooth space of gum that ran from where the upper left lateral incisor all the way to where the upper left second molar should have been, and checked his watch once again. It was at least two minutes since the last time he'd looked.

"Fingers!" Beetlejuice turned with a start to see his brother, King Smurf, standing, a frustrated look on his blue face, "what the fuck you doin'? They'll get here when they fuckin' get here! Come and fuckin' dance yer daft prick!

King Smurf
Real Name: Richard 'Dickfingers' Fing
Age: 27
Occupation: Cycle shop manager
Likes: Good quality tuneage & Dancing
Dislikes: Music snobs & Ignorance
Most Likely to Dance to: Darude – Sandstorm

He's pulled his brother from the lobby because he's bored. Jackson is away in the toilets, having clearly not learned his lesson from the Wetherspoons debacle. As soon as they got here he was complaining about the music, asking why they couldn't go to a decent indie rock club instead, somewhere that each tune wouldn't sound exactly the same as the last one. This is the standard argument. Jackson will always declare that it's all the same shit, by a different DJ, asking how much skill a man actually needs to make the noise that they do. King Smurf will always ask why he has to be like that, it's his opinion that the world wouldn't be right if everybody was into the same stuff. He doesn't mind the music that Jackson will force into their ears on a regular basis, it's not stuff that he would choose himself, but King Smurf respects musicians for getting up from their arses and doing something. Besides, DJs did need a huge amount of talent to do what they did, otherwise it would indeed simply be a mish mash of noise. A good DJ would know when to build the noise, and when to drop the beat, and bring it slowly back up before it kicks in and his, or indeed her, audience would go mental. A good DJ knows exactly what a raver needs, and wants. An excellent DJ will fulfil their needs without fail.

"Fuckin' tune!" King Smurf shouts into the air as Fedde LeGrande instructs that they should put their hands up for the city of Detroit, he pulls the arm of his brother and drags him roughly from where he stands, weaves them through the crowd, like a half bright blue, half pale white snake. Already King Smurf holds his free arms aloft, pumps it into the air to the *thump thump thump thump* of the beat. He's in his element, he loves this tune. He's still got a hold on Beetlejuice, who's doing his best to replicate his brother's rhythm but the truth of it is that he was hanging around the bad luck queue when they were handing out rhythm, so as it is he resembles an electrocuted ragdoll, his knees bending to an imaginary off-beat entirely out of sync with his flailing arm. The worst thing is the look of pure concentration in his face, like he's trying to figure a particularly hard sum, and the answer's literally right on the tip of his tongue. King Smurf smiles at his brother affectionately as they find a small pocket of space beside a pair of brunette girls, both borderline underage, but well into the tunes. As the beat drops off one of the girls lets out an enthusiastic *whoooo!* and smiles his way, King Smurf smiles back and waits for Fedde to bring it back up. Arms rise from the crowd, fingers tickle at the laser light that rolls above them. They are unified in their love of the tune. As the tune increases in tempo the strobe kicks in *put your hands up put your hands up put your hand up put your hands up* hands are up, the crowd begins to jump, they know what's coming *put your put your put your put your put put put put put put put put* it's coming, they can feel it. Then it hits. *Put your hands up for Detroit.* Boom. The crowd go mental, even Beetlejuice with his epileptic flailing is fitting in with the rest of them, and for once tonight, he has a smile on his stupid face.

Through the waving arms King Smurf sees the veritable smacked arse that is the gurning face of Jackson, the miserable fucker. He's standing between two couples, sucking the faces off of each other, between the lusty balls he is the spare prick. King Smurf beckons him over and on to dance floor but he can tell from the face that he'd have more of a chance if he were on a mission to find rocking-horse shit. He'd rather martyr himself and have something to blame everybody for when they're in the taxi home, tell them all how much fun he *didn't* have. But King Smurf will be ready for him, it was *his* fault that they've had to split up, if he'd kept out of trouble he might have had a chance to argue his case for going to a different club, but he didn't, and now it is what it is. No point grumbling about it, you have to make the best of a bad situation.

***

We're at the door of this house, and Sasha's unlocked herself from Justin long enough to finger around inside in her little, tiny, *miniscule* bag and pull some keys out. There's some music coming from inside the house, and it sounds like decent stuff they'll be playing. She's trying to get the key in the door, but each jab at the hole comes out unsuccessful, it's probably a combination of being drunk, and the fact that Justin's hands are pawing away at her arsecheeks, and she's giggling like fuck---This is mad as fuck---the strong smell of weed floats through from the kitchen, and I'm feeling really good so I have no qualms about going in there and introducing myself in the form of a nod and a smile. There's two fellas in here, obviously students, one of them's wearing an orange woolly hat, with the ear flaps and braided tassles hanging off. I like those hats. He's in some sort of dialogue with his mate, a fella with a Creedence Clearwater Revival T-shirt on, which already marks him as a cool motherfucker in my book, for sure, you'll not find a Creedence T-shirt in fucking Topman, not like the Ramones and Led Zep T-shirts that are doing the rounds nowadays. Piss me off them. Anyway, they're talking about Star Wars, or Star Trek, or some other shit, which isn't my cup of tea but these cats have got a spliff on the go and I want in on that shit---

----

--------------------------------fuckin' reyt do this,
everybody's so---

---line of
charlie on the back of a CD case, it's some local band,
The Fall of the Union, and this kid's telling me that it's
his band, enthusing the fuck out of it, telling me it's a
fusion of spaced out shoegaze and drum and bass.
"We're like, early Verve meets Pendulum, mate, you'd
have to hear it to believe it," he's saying, his hands
reaching out for a grab of the case, but he can fucking
wait, I've got a powdery ridge of coke to get up into
my snout first. Across the room Justin's still got the

girl Sasha on his lap, honestly that kid's defo getting balls deep in that lass tonight, I wouldn't be surprised if there was a little longer term romance on the cards. I'm sitting with my back to the brown sofa, which I have to say is in very good nick considering that this is a shared student house. For sure, I'm thinking there should be a million fag burns in it by now, but they're very restrained these kids. Smoking is confined to the kitchen, with the back door open, but all other drugs are okay in the lounge. There's a cool looking Bose docking system in the corner, with an iPod sticking out the top of it, I'm itching to get up and see what's on it but we've not been here long, I don't wanna start hijacking the tunes. Well, I *do* want to, but there's an etiquette and I'm not *that* much of a cunt that I'd totally break that, I mean, for sure, I start fiddling with their tunes and the cock blockers'll be out in force, then that might jeopardise my chances of getting a bit of action with the lovely Cassie, and we do *not* want that. Too much effort put in already to fuck that up. Other than us lot there's a few people floating about the house, it's a very cool affair, seriously, they're obviously used to randoms coming and going, 'cause they're paying us no mind at all. We've got DJ Shadow coming from the speakers, and I'm already picking at the lip of my baggy, and tapping another couple of lines out, one for me and one for the delightful Cassie. She's all over it like a tramp on a pasty like a seasoned professional, which impresses me no end, then she's down on the floor, her arms around my neck and her lips are all over mine. Her leg shifts slightly to nudge against my hand, as if to wake it up, and suddenly it's slithering up the inside of her thigh, my thumb strumming against it like I were playing a lovely tanner guitar. She gasps, and slams the thighs shut on my trapped hand. I'm wondering if she's offended by my being forward, but there's this dirty little grin on her face. "Not here sunshine, come on."

Then she's up on her feet, both hands pulling at my arm, hoisting me up onto my feet. I look to my boys, but Dicko's making a point of looking at his watch, and Justin's lost in Sasha, it's a shame they couldn't be upstanding in their support of my forthcoming sexual endeavours, but fuck it, I'm getting laid. You fucking dancer!

The Incredible Hulk
Real Name: Joseph "Joe" Thompson
Age: 26
Occupation: Bus Driver
Likes: His mum's Sunday dinners & The nap that follows
Dislikes: Working on a Sunday & Cheeky kids
Most Likely to Dance to: Take That - Never Forget

The boys have found themselves in the Lower Briggate area of the city, and found a lively spacious bar. The music pumps through both the crowd in here and the thudding floor which sends satisfactory vibrations right the way up The Incredible Hulk's feet, legs, and right into his cock and balls. The clientele here are friendly, and flamboyant. He's not in any way perturbed to note he and the others seem to have stumbled into the gay district, given the high ratio of drag queens to men dressed as actual men. Hulk doesn't mind these places, as they're less likely to throw up the possibility of a scrap for one, and for another, his cousin Sam is gay, and he has enjoyed many a night out with him back in Sheffield. Hulk is proud of his own open-mindedness, and wears it like a badge much the same as the lesbian who's shuffling past him is wearing the biggest strap-on he's ever seen. He's never been to Ibiza but he imagines that these places are the closest thing to there that you could get back in England, with the flamboyancy, and the show people which ply their trade. Outside the window a pair of stilts, attached to a bald man covered from head to toe in glittery golden paint, resembling a gay version of an Oscar, but on stilts. Following closely behind him another golden man blows fires across the landscape of the huge window. Hulk laughs, he could never be that way out, he likes tits far too much, but he can't help but admire the courage, and blatant in-your-face attitude of those that are. From his vantage point at the bar he sees Hitler and Superman standing in the corner, uneasily, but still having a good time in the corner. Hitler especially is the kind of man who thinks that every gay in the place is attracted to him, wants to ride his arse like The Lone Ranger on Silver. He's the alpha male who'll loudly declare that it's *Arses to the wall time lads,* making not just an ignorant show of himself, but also of those with him. Superman will laugh loudly, and ignorantly, and Hulk will display the behaviours of the kid in a gang of bullies with split allegiances. His friend is being picked on, and for fear of persecution he will laugh along, but at the same time his eyes will apologise to the victim. Today however, he's loving the atmosphere, the drugs are riding high in his bloodstream, and nothing is going to bring him down.

"Fuckin' love it here!" he enthuses to Hitler, whose, Hulk is surprised to note, own discriminations are floating uncharacteristically deep below the surface, they've had a brilliant night so far, and none of them are in any mood to spoil it. Hitler nods with an inane grin.

"Mint innit? You see that fella wi' tits? Fuckin' bonkers mate."

A trio of attractive girls appear from across the bar, and make a show of admiring the outfits, especially that of The Incredible Hulk.

"Ladies," he smiles, and shouts over Kylie Minogue failing to get the object of her desire out of her head, the girls coo and cluck around him, one especially catches his eyes. She's tall and slim, unfeasibly attractive. Her bright green hair shimmers beneath the disco lights of the bar, and her pale face seems flawless. The others find their personal favourite to flirt with, Hitler has attached himself to the smallest of the trio, an oriental looking, and petite work of art. Superman half-heartedly chats to the remaining girl, a slightly heavier set, mutton dressed as lamb type. The pub melts away and Hulk stares into the eyes of the green haired beauty, his gaze wandering down her body, drinking in the delightful curves, down her long, slender legs, and back up to her eyes. She gestures wildly about her hair, and then points to Hulk, but he's not getting it. He makes an exaggerated shrug, mouthing *what?* at her. She has a look of mock frustration, places a hand expertly and delicately onto her hip, tilting her head as she rests her weight on one leg. She points back to her hair, shouting something, and then back to the Hulk, shouting something else. He knows what she's talking about but still shrugs, and beckons her closer. He wants to smell her, to feel her breath on his neck. He wants to have her close enough to slip a hand onto her waist, to feel her skin. She does as she is bidden and draws closer. She smells fantastic, he knows this perfume as Issy Miyake. There's a regular girl who gets his bus in the mornings that he's grown fond of, and speaks to every day, she wears this same perfume, and he's asked her what it is before. He loves the smell, so fruity.

"My hair," she calls into his ear. The sensation of the tingle in his neck makes a beeline for his balls, and awakens the blood in his cock, all he wants right now is to take this girl in his arms, carry her out of this place, and fuck the hell out of her, that look in her eyes, it says that she wants the same, "it's the same colour as you."

He nods.

"It suits you," he says, "you're fit as fuck."

She giggles, and if she's in any way embarrassed by his forwardness she's not showing it, her stance shifts slightly, safe in the knowledge that she's snared him.

"So are you," she confirms, then slowly runs her tongue up his neck below the ear. Superman and Hitler no longer exist. The girls they're chatting to neither. The grand show which goes on outside is nothing. There's just The Incredible Hulk and this green haired succubus. He almost feels faint from the lack of blood anywhere in his body except his massive hard on. After he adjusts, and slides the thing upwards, against his belly, Hulk pushes himself closer into her body, pressing his erection against her leg. This green haired beauty pulls away, and looks down with a smile, before drawing closer to his ear once again.

"Do you want to fuck?"

Hulk cannot help but nod with the eagerness of a child who has been asked if he wants a screwball ice cream for the first time, after having been informed for so long that he wasn't allowed to have one since it contained a bubble gum on which he might choke to death, and he turns to Hitler.

"I'll see you in a bit mate," he says with a wink and a flash of teeth, then without a second thought he follows the wiggling, and ridiculously edible behind of the green haired beauty.

They haven't said much to each other as they reach a darkened alleyway close to the railway arches, his newest object of desire leading the way, the pair of them stopping periodically to kiss passionately. The sounds of the city rock into the air, wailing of boys and girls partying their Friday night away, the techno combines with rock music combines with trance combines with bubblegum pop to pollute the air in the most musical way possible. As they approach a dank archway the green haired girl spins on her heels and leans against the sweating wall, pulling The Incredible Hulk toward her with intent, jams her tongue deep into his throat and the pair become an almighty, slithering creature, arms everywhere. Hulk's hands glide over her small breasts, roughly squeezing them, searching for erect nipples through the light material of her short dress. The green haired girl slides her own hand up the impressive length of his shaft, pulling it from his torn shorts, the pink skin betraying his green torso. She drops to her knees, her hands clamped tight around his backside, and puts the thing into her mouth. Hulk's mouth drops open as the girl expertly works his shaft with her tongue, and fights the gagging reflex from the bulb of his cock forcing her throat further open. Suddenly she stops, and looks up to him.

"I want it in my pussy," she says, and doesn't need to ask him twice, he pulls her up from her knees, kisses her hard on the mouth, his hand slides up the thigh of her skirt, trying to force the thing up over her arse so he can rip down her pants, but she stops him, and pulls away, the pair of them combining to create a breathless beast, "no," she says, "from behind."

Al Capone

He awoke with a gasp. An awful throbbing sensation in his throat. What was the last thing he remembered? The needle. *Welcome to the AIDS club.* The tramp had taken him by surprise and punched him hard in the face, knocking him to the ground. *Welcome to the AIDS club.* He'd been held to the ground by the boot of the kid crushing against his throat, choking him. He'd struggled against it, grabbing at the leg but it was in vain, he had been too strong. Al Capone had blacked out before long and woken here and now. He tried to swallow but it was agony. There was a weird cooling sensation on the skin of his face. Blood, half dried, like a dark red version of the PVA glue he remembered coating his fingers in, and then peeling away once it had dried. He moved, aware that he was laid upon something. Bin bags. The dirty fucker had assaulted him and dragged him out of the way. *Welcome to the AIDS club.* With a start his hands darted to his gut, where the kid had stabbed him. Nothing there. Had he imagined that part? He'd been pretty drunk. Unsteadily he rose to his feet, like a new born giraffe, fighting the urge to throw up, and looked to his gut, his hands clawing desperately at the white Egyptian cotton shirt he'd paid a fortune for. It was there, small but definitely there. A speck of deep red soaked into the material. *Welcome. To the fucking. AIDS club.* Capone searched for his phone, he needed The Pimp. Jesus. Christ, he'd even take Hitler at that point. An ear, a face, anybody to tell him that this wasn't happening. The trouser pockets were empty, as were the ones in his jacket. Panic stricken he turned, pulled the big bags that had been his bed for the last, however many minutes, or hours. Nothing. The bags tore upon impact as they hit the road behind him, scattering discarded food, napkins, and paper drinks cups across the concrete. The further he dug the more panic stricken he became. There was nothing there. The kid had cleaned him out. The hundreds of quid in pound coins were gone, his phone, his wallet, even his keys. Suddenly he's aware of the cool breeze over his feet. The scruffy little cunt had even taken his shoes. *Welcome to the AIDS club.* But more than anything else, if what he had done was true, he'd taken Capone's life. He was standing here in his socks, alone and without means of calling home, to his mum, with whom he lived since she did everything for him, asked for scant board for his lodgings, allowed him to put thousands and thousands of pounds away in the bank. But the kid had his bank card. *For fuck's sake.* He had no means of getting a train home, he had no idea where in this fucking city he was, so no means of getting back to the taxi, if it hadn't gone already. Capone roared into the night out of pure frustration, fighting through the agony in his throat. If he were a lesser man he might have dropped to his knees, head in his hands, sobbing uncontrollably at the futility of his situation. Capone, however, placed a great pride in the fact that he hadn't shed a tear since he'd broken his ankle playing football for the school team over sixteen years ago, and his dad had cuffed him round the earhole for being a fanny. He even remembered the date, April twentieth, nineteen eighty nine, it was part of his own personal patter, a statistic that he kept internal, to make him feel better about himself when others around him went to shit. He'd not even wept when his dad passed away in the mid-nineties, his dad having hammered it into him that crying was for gays and girls. Such was his fear of the man that he'd worried that he'd be watching up from hell, ready to catch the tear as it dropped from his chin, the *psssssst* as it hit his burning hand, which would curl round to form a fist, and then whack him full in the face. He'd never actually hit Capone in his time on Earth, but the threat of it simmered beneath the surface their whole lives.

Capone took stock of the situation. *It is what it is.* He needed to get to a hospital, find out what the shit head had really pumped into his bloodstream. *Welcome to the AIDS club.* That phrase. It swirled around his headspace like, a glob of deep, dark green snot, spat into a sink, rotating the plughole in the running water, refusing to drop down the drain and out of his life. He heard voices. They were the voices of two girls, holding on to each other for support in the midst of their inebriation, not helped any by the unnecessarily high shoes they were wearing.

"Girls!" he called, stepping tentatively, but as quickly as he could toward them. One of them paused, wobbled, focussed on the bloody, shoeless mess that was tramping toward her, and then continued on her way, "Please! Stop!"

He could feel every bump, crack, and pebble against the soles of his feet against the path as he picked up his pace. Pressing down hard he stepped onto something, something sharp, but he couldn't stop, he needed help, and he needed it now.

Big Poppa Smurf

"Yeah, we've been going a while now, supported We Are Scientists when they played too."

"Really? That's cool, you must be doing well."

"Not as well as we'd like, nobody really knows us outside of Yorkshire, doesn't translate to sales in the charts y'know? Still got to work and all that."

Big Poppa Smurf has unhooked himself from Sasha, and is in dialogue with Lenny, the kid from the band who was so eager to get his music heard earlier on. The pair of them are in the kitchen with The Pimp, and Lenny is carefully constructing a three skin spliff as he speaks. He seems a genuinely good kid, and the enthusiasm he has for his subject matter is infectious. Big Poppa Smurf has racked up three lines of coke, and swoops down onto the largest of the three before passing the rolled up purple queenie to The Pimp, who has lightened up somewhat in the last half an hour.

"Love to be able to play an instrument, like, drums or summat like that," says Big Poppa Smurf, his finger picking gently at the rim of his nostril, searching for stray crumbs of coke. His finger finds a sharp edge and pulls the thing away, allowing him to examine it, and, once he's happy that it *is* coke, and not a big crusty greenie, places it onto his tongue, delighting in the sensation as the tip goes numb.

"Lenny," says The Pimp, attracting the attention of the musician, holding out the note for him to take a go on his line. Lenny gratefully takes it and returns to skinning up, "Jackson's a good guitarist though, really good."

Big Poppa Smurf nods enthusiastically and turns to Lenny.

"Yeah, one of the lads who came out with us, Andy, brilliant guitarist, seriously, quickest fingers I've ever seen."

Lenny licks the length of the part rolled spliff and twists it, before flicking it expertly through the air and catching the roached end in his lips, lighting it steadily.

"So what bands are you into then?" he asks through the croaked voice of a man holding good quality weed smoke in his lungs for the longest time possible, he's directed this question to The Pimp, having already had a similar conversation with Big Poppa Smurf. The Pimp contemplates the question, giving it a long *hmmmmm* in the process.

"All sorts."

Big Poppa Smurf hates this type of answer, he thinks it's a cop out, *all sorts,* it could mean anything. He knows for a fact that The Pimp loves The Clash and Ramones. He could have divulged that he had a soft spot for Bowling For Soup. But no, he says *all sorts.* He doesn't say anything though, it would be bad sportsmanship to pull up his mate and show off in front of a relative stranger. In front of Jesus or one of the others then yes, that would be funny, but in front of Lenny it's a whole different game. For Lenny, however, he would be fair game, and Big Poppa Smurf can sense from his knowing grin that he knows this too.

"Allsorts, yeah, I know their stuff," he grins, a mischievous glint in his eyes, smoke billowing from his mouth. Big Poppa Smurf struggles to stifle a snigger and The Pimp looks at the pair of them, his mind working on a response, eventually he shakes his head with a smile.

"Get fucked," he laughs, taking the joint from Lenny and taking a strong pull on its arse. Big Poppa Smurf can feel vibrations in the room that are so good that even The Beach Boys would struggle to contain their envy, and Mike Love might feel moved to leave a flaming bag of dog shit on their doorstep before ringing the doorbell and scarpering to the ethereal soundtrack of Brian Wilson insulting them in a delightful falsetto tone.

***

Her dress is up around her waist and my fingers are eagerly picking at the edges of her little pants, grappling to pull them down over her gorgeous arse and down past her thighs. Her hands are wrestling against the bed sheet which is doubling as a gown, desperate to get themselves in direct contact with my cock, which feels that skin-on-skin contact is just as crucial. I love that feeling of a woman's hands when they first cop a hold of my member----------------------
----

--------------------trousers strewn onto the floor on top of her dress. I'm looking down at her, she's smooth as fuck, and I mean *all over.* I kiss her lips but my mouth already wants to head down south, so I make it worth her while by trailing my tongue down her neck-------
----

--want to go
further down but I can't get enough of her nipples,
they're like sexy little jelly tots, and my fingers tease
between her legs, stroking her thighs and she's--------

-----------------she gasps, and her fingers grab at my
hair as my tongue gently flicks at-------------------------

--grinding her clit against my face which is sopping
wet by now---

------------------bucking against me and I'm pulling
myself up, guiding my hard on toward her still
twitching fanny, pushing myself against her, and it
seems like she's still constricted 'cause it's a struggle
to get inside, but I'm pushing, and pushing. Suddenly
I'm in, like the gates opened for me, welcoming me
inside her like a bunch of munchkins welcoming
Dorothy to the wonderful world of Oz, and I'm going
for it but something doesn't feel right. It hurts. She's
totally in the moment and still bucking violently

against me but that niggling ache in my cock won't go away.

"Stop, stop a minute," I gasp, and her face goes all confused 'cause she was well into it.

"What's up?" she asks breathlessly, "just fuck me!"

"I just need to check something," I'm saying, up on my elbows but my cock is still gripped tight by her lady garden, and I'm clumsily clambering up onto my knees, and as I withdraw my cock I look down to see the carnage. It's absolutely coated in blood, and it's still fucking dripping. Cassie's face is probably whiter than mine as she sees the gruesome pork sword I'm currently waving in her direction, and she's pushing herself back against the headboard.

"Oh God, what have you done to me?" she's squealing, her hands grabbing at her hole, pulling her bloody fingers away and just staring at it.

"I don't think it's you," I say, as I pull my quickly withering cock up, and inspect the underside. The blood is still streaming from the bulb, like a deep red spring from some obscure source in the side of a purple meaty mountain, but on this occasion I know *exactly* where it's coming from. My banjo string has fucking snapped in two. The little fleshy sock suspender that's spent my whole life keeping my foreskin attached to my bell end has been decimated and is streaming worse than an eyeball in an onion factory. For sure, I feel sick as fuck.

"I've snapped me fuckin' banjo," I say, and she's just looking confused.

"Your what?"

"My banjo, my banjo, I've snapped me fucking banjo string, this is sore as fuck!"

I'm up off the bed now, there's this massive, fuck off great shiny crimson wet patch on the sheets, it looks like I've stabbed the fuck out of her fanny with a knife, like that badass strap-on that the fella gets forced to fuck that hooker with from the film Seven, and she's been bled dry all over her bed linen. That's how bad it looks.

"Have you got any tissue or a towel or owt?"

She's up looking now, and you can see the apprehension in her eyes as she spots this towel on the radiator, all pure white and fluffy--------------------
----

----

absolutely drenched in blood, and I'm hobbling down the stairs in my T-shirt and trainers, Cassie's got my gown scrunched up in her arms, following me and whilst I'm numbed from the booze, drugs and just out-and-out surrealism of it all I can still feel the sore in my cock. Cassie's giving it the *oh God, oh God* behind me and I'm calling out for Dicko or Justin to come and help me. They appear together from the kitchen, followed by the kid from the band, and I can smell weed again, God, I'd kill for a go on the spliff----
----

--------------sitting in the kitchen chair, and Sasha's on her knees in front of me, holding on to my cock, and I'm struggling to keep my erection from re-surfacing and I'm thinking of my gran having a three-way with my mum and dad, I'm thinking that Freddy Mercury rocks up and gives my dad a lap dance, and it's slowly, slowly doing the trick, which is good, because I *cannot* get another hard on. Then from the

cupboard emerges Cassie, and she's got this bottle of
something--

--------------------------------sharp intake of breath as
Sasha's holding my flaccid cock upright and Cassie's
spraying disinfectant TCP onto my ripped open bell
end. I open my eyes and beyond my pair of sexy
nurses there's Dicko and Justin struggling to hold in
their laughter. I know if the shoe was on the other
foot, or if the snapped banjo was on another cock I'd
be laughing too, after the initial crossed legs moment.
But, for sure, the shoe is on *my* fucking foot, and this
is awful. The other lads and girls from the party are
all gathered round too, and I'm the big show tonight.
Cassie sprays again, and then dabs at my aching bulb.
I think the little lad is in shock just now 'cause the
pain's subsiding.
"Okay, hold it there," she says, her hands tentatively
edging away, her face just dripping with genuine
sympathy, which is a stark contrast to the smirking,
piss-taking face of Dicko behind her. I'll kill the cunt, I
really will. I can't believe I'm sat here, bollocks out,
and two women have had their hands all over my
cock and it was all for the wrong reasons. I should be
spraying my muck all over Cassie's divine tits but I'm
not, I've sprayed blood from my snapped banjo string
all over both her, and her sheets, and now she's
returned the favour by spraying disinfectant all over
the wound.
"How you doing mate?" says Dicko, drawing closer to
slap me on the back.
"I think the phrase is *I'll laugh about this one day.*"

Justin has a little chuckle at that one and holds the spliff my way, so I'm gently holding the cotton against my cock with one hand, and reaching out with the other.

"You'll be laughin' about it in no time, here, get your laughin' tackle round that," he says, then this cheeky flash crosses his face, and his mind starts ticking, you know that that's what's happening 'cause his eyes start running from left to right, like he's reading summat, then his hands come up, like he's conducting an invisible orchestra.

"And it seems to me, you'll live your life, with a damaged banjo string," he's singing to me as if he's Elton fucking John singing *Candle in the Wind*! The cheeky twat! The rest of the room erupts into laughter, and I'm still here holding my cock in one hand and a spliff to my lips. I shake my head and laugh 'cause that actually was quite quick, the bastard, it has to be said that I do have some funny mates. The laughter subsides, and I'm still shaking my head.

"Fuck off," I say, "you daft cunt," I say, "do me a fucking line," I say, and I blow a lung full of smoke in his direction before I pass the spliff to Cassie, our very own cock-injury-specialising Florence Nightingale.

Hitler

He's been chatting to the girl about not much for about half an hour and he thinks that she's like a perfect china doll, twisting her hair and tilting her head as she shouts over the music. He's entranced by her eyes, the way they blink slowly when she smiles. Her bright white teeth. She's the very pretty type of Oriental girl, very petite, very flawless. Hitler loves

Asian girls. His finds that, when they are the pretty
ones, then they are the most beautiful women on the
planet. With the MDMA coursing through his blood
he feels comfortable enough to tell Xu this. Xu. *A
beautiful name for a beautiful girl.* She took the well-
meant, casually racist compliment in her stride,
twisted her hair some more, tilted her head further
still, brought her foot up behind her as she reached to
place a kiss on his cheek. Hitler is in love. He drinks
her beauty in through his puppy dog eyes. Hulk has
yet to return. Superman has his tongue slithering
deep down the throat of his own personal beauty. His
hands clamped firmly on her firm round arse. Hitler
reflects that Superman does have an eye for the
larger ladies, he always says that he wants something
to grab a hold of, that sex with skinny girls is like
fucking a ladder. Hitler doesn't care for anything
right now, he just wants to drown in the huge brown
pools of Xu's eyes.
"You're so," he starts, and pauses for effect, "*fucking*,"
he emphasises for further effect, "beautiful."
Xu smiles again.
"Yes, you said."
"But I just can't get over how, beautiful, you are.
You're perfect."
"And you're on drugs yeah?"
Hitler blinks, nods, smiles. Xu returns his smile.
"Then you are looking through rose tinted
spectacles."
Hitler shakes his head, and goes to speak but Xu
places a dainty finger on his lips, reaches up once
again to kiss his cheek, which is becoming a smeared
pink blotch from the repeated applications of lipstick.
"You are sweet," she says.
Suddenly the spell is broken by a heavy green hand
planted down upon his shoulder. Hitler turns to see

The Incredible Hulk, wide eyed, panic stricken. Hitler cheers and plants a kiss on his big green face.

"This boy here," he says to Xu, "this boy here is my hero. I love him. He's a beautiful man."

The Incredible Hulk doesn't play up on this, he clearly has something on his mind, Hitler ignores the panic.

"He's the best boy I've ever known, he's beautiful. You're beautiful mate."

"I need a word," says The Incredible Hulk, "I mean, now."

Already Hulk is out of the door, and Hitler feels a mild concern for his friend, but still he doesn't want to tear himself away from Xu. He can feel the burn of Hulk's stare through the window so he excuses himself and follows the green superhero.

"What's up my man?" Hitler says as he approaches Hulk.

"Mate, that bird," he says, and swallows down what he needs to say, his hand rubs the back of his painted head.

"Yeah, she was lovely mate, proper lovely," Hitler gushes, but from the look of his friend's face he feels he'd be inclined to disagree, "mate, what's up?"

"It were all going fine, she were suckin' me off, then she tells me to stick it in her pussy, her words, she says *put it in my pussy,* so I'm well up for that, and she tells me to put it in from behind, right?"

"Right, nowt wrong wi' that."

"You'd think wunt yer? Well, I've got me soldier out and she guides it in, and she's proper pushing on to me, moaning like fuck, keeps saying *fuck my pussy, fuck my pussy,* and it starts to get on my tits, but I keep pumpin', an' as soon as she comes I shoot me muck up into her."

"Good lad. So what's up for fuck's sake?"

Hitler is tiring of the conversation, he doesn't want Xu to disappear, he wants to continue to drown in her eyes.

"Well," says Hulk, still struggling for the words, "when I pulled out, I had shit on me cock."

"Eh?"

"That's what I thought."

"She said to fuck her pussy!"

"Exactly! So I tuck my cock away an' spins her around, asks her what she's playin' at."

"And?"

"Well, this is the thing, she didn't get a chance to answer me 'cause I notice that she's got a cock herself, honestly, it were bigger than mine, an' I just panicked, I fucked her off."

"Fuck off!"

"No really, I've just left her. We need to fuck off before she comes back."

Hitler understands The Incredible Hulk's concern, and he fully appreciates his anxiety, but something niggles him in this story, and it's growing into something truly hilarious.

"Wait, why do you keep callin' him a *her?*" he laughs, *"*You just fucked a ladyboy mate."

Hulk shakes his head in agreement, and sighs with a resigned labour.

"I know, can't believe I din't click. I tell you what though, he were a crackin' shag."

At this point Superman joins them outside the door, closely followed by Xu and her own friend.

"Where's Krystle?" asks the heavier set girl, whose name entirely eludes Hitler, but is starting to look just ever so slightly masculine in the street light. With a heavy heart he begins to concede that Xu has also taken on a man-like form, albeit a very pretty one, beautiful even. The concept alone confuses Hitler, who's still riding high on an ecstasy buzz.

"I'm sorry," says Hulk, "I just panicked."

"What did you do?" asks Xu, a fearful look in her, his, *its* eyes. A look that said that they'd been here before. Duped an unsuspecting yet complicit bloke into sex. Maybe not even duped, they had a right to live their lives as they wanted, to look as attractive as they could, if a man finds them fit then does that say more about him than it does the ladyboy? Then to take a beating when the reality came crashing into the situation like a train, it just wasn't right. He was guilty of occasional homophobia, he accepted that, but the drug induced flushes of love for the beauty of Xu make him hate himself more than anything.

"Nothing," says The Incredible Hulk, "I just ran."

"Where is she?"

"Dunno," he says, his face displays a mixed up bucket of emotions, the most notable to Hitler being confusion, disappointment, anguish.

Xu takes off in the direction of the railway arches, followed by the mate. Hitler shakes his head, but he needs to see that face again, so he also heads off in the same direction, with Superman and Hulk in tow. Behind him Superman is asking what the fuck is happening. Hulk tells him that he doesn't want to know.

Al Capone

"Stop! Please"

Al Capone limps into the road, arms flailing. One car, a black Kia Cee'd, swerves to avoid him, horn honking furiously. The driver, a middle aged bloke with a salt and pepper dashed crop of short hair, offers him nothing but an angry arm, silent profanities through his window but he doesn't stop to either help, or perhaps more thankfully, physically attack Capone. The car races off into the distance and Capone turns to try to flag down the next vehicle. It's a taxi. The car slows to a halt, the driver shrouded in darkness, and Capone pulls the rear door open, sliding thankfully in behind the man at the wheel.

"Hospital please, be quick!" he gasps at the back of his head.

The red door clicks, and the red light illuminates to indicate that the doors are locked and the taxi chugs into life. The driver says nothing, but his eyes flicker to the rear view mirror to consider his latest passenger. Capone resembles a businessman from the twenties, but one who seems to have had too much of a good time, and is dishevelled from its effects. He's ripping off his sock, slapping it against the leather of the seat, and he pulls his foot up with a sharp grimace, investigating the sore of his injured foot. The driver cannot see it, but there's a shard of glass, maybe an inch squared, half of that inch is embedded deep into Al Capone's foot. He cannot believe that this night has turned out the way it has. The rest of them, Jesus, The Pimp, fucking *Hitler*, will be lapping this up when they hear about it, he reflects. *Welcome to the AIDS club.* Maybe not. Maybe they'd be sympathetic to his plight, surely to God they'd be sympathetic. Only a real scumbag would find humour in what he has experienced so far, even his worst enemy couldn't help but feel for him. His fingers pick at the edge of the glass in his foot, he hopes that it's not an iceberg situation, where the majority of the shard is inside him, and what he's picking at isn't just the tip. The freshly created mouth of skin around the shard is hungry though, it resists his gentle tugs and the pain of each endeavour rips through his leg, through his balls and into his stomach. Capone doubles over in pain, gasping for air. He knows that his hobbling has forced the shard of glass deeper in, and it is unlikely that he'll pluck up the strength to remove it himself. Resigned to this fact he leans back, pulling up his shirt, taking a brief second to consider the spot of red around the front. *Welcome to the AIDS club.* His skin seems to have sealed back up around the slight puncture from where the filthy disease ridden needle entered his body. Then something occurs to him. In his desperation he realises that he has no money to pay for this taxi.

He wrestles his injured foot underneath him and drops heavily to his knees in the cabin at the back, his face drawing closer to the Perspex panel which separates the driver from his fares, and his mind runs through the various ways of broaching the subject. He could remain true to form and aggressively demand that the driver lets him off, he could give his name, and address, and hope that the guy is sympathetic, or he could just beg.

"Um, 'scuse me," he says, his lips pressed sheepishly against the communication portal which consists of a circle which consists of a hundred tiny other circles cut into the plastic panel. The driver's head turns slightly to the sound, but his eyes remain on the road. He says nothing.

"Sorry to bother you," says Capone, his heart giddy as the bright light of the hospital draws into view, *salvation,* he is within touching distance of help. Of a man who will declare that his night has all just been one cruel joke, and that he can continue his life as carefree as ever, that he can go back to making money, spending money, flashing his money around to show everybody exactly how much more of it that he has than everybody else. The taxi swings right to make its ascent to the hospital grounds.

"I were robbed," he says, "I don't have any money," he continues, "if there's any way you could just let me off, I really need medical help, I was attacked, and I got stabbed, and-"

The hospital comes, and then goes, as the taxi speeds up.

"What? What are you doing? Please!"

Desperation creeps into Al's tone, and he watches the hospital gradually disappear behind them, before turning back to the panel.

"Please, I'm sorry, I need a doctor," he cries, panic stricken. His already overworked brain struggles to process the latest turn of events. Just two minutes ago he was within touching distance of help, or salvation. Now, however, the glimmer of hope he'd previously had is being gradually strangled, and wrestled from his desperate grasp. His emotion roars like a train through the stations of panic, and fear, and begin to slow at its final destination, fury. Al Capone slams his hand against the Perspex panel, his face twisted, and gnarled, his teeth bared like those of a dog whose food is under threat.

"Stop the fuckin' car you mental cunt!" he bellows from the back of the taxi but to no avail, again he strikes the plastic, the driver barely registers a reaction, "I need a fuckin' doctor!"

As the city begins to shrink around them, the spaces where there were office blocks begin to make way for lower level garages, car dealerships, bed and carpet showrooms. Those buildings disappear too, and they're in a residential area. Terraced housing, made of dark red bricks, boarded windows and graffiti, estates that have been starved of meaningful existence. Al Capone has spent the last five minutes hammering the plastic panel, wailing until his throat his raw, offering threats of violence, of the deaths of the driver's wife and children, of his pets. All of them attracting no flicker of a response from the seemingly emotionless driver. Capone is desperate. He's been forced to walk the streets of a strange city alone, admittedly through his own reactionary tendency, been attacked, robbed, stabbed with a contaminated syringe, cut open his foot and now has a shard of glass wedged deep into his flesh, and to top it all off he has been kidnapped by a crazed taxi driver. Al Capone doesn't think that the night could possibly get any worse, the driver can do as he pleases. His fury subsides to acceptance, and he sits back in the seat of the car, never taking his eyes from those of the driver through the rear view mirror. No, it's only as he's hurtling through the air and face first into the plastic panel as the driver smashes the taxi directly into the arse end of a stationary truck, and his lights begin to dim and he drifts sadly into unconsciousness as the driver rips open the back door, and drags him from the cab that Al Capone realises that his night could, and indeed *will*, get a hell of a lot worse.

Jackson

This was possibly the worst stag do he'd ever been on. He'd been dragged from the pub and blamed for the following split up they'd been forced into. He'd found himself standing alone outside the shit hole of a nightclub, smoking a cig and listening to the inane ramblings of a pair of pissed girls. One, a fairy-winged slag with curly brown hair and an extraordinarily long head chuntered to her shorter, fatter friend. They resembled caked-in-makeup real life versions of Bert and Ernie from Sesame Street.

"He don't need to know though does he?" said the shorter girl.

"But he'll know, all his mates were there Chloe, he'll kill me," whined the other, "I don't even know why I let him finger me."

Jackson chuckled through the cigarette smoke he exhaled, drawing a look from the girls. One of confusion which evolved gradually into disdain. The girl with the long head scowled right at him as she stepped toward him.

"What you fuckin' laughin' at dickhead?"

"What? Nowt!" said Jackson, he'd had enough trouble tonight.

"You fuckin' were! You were fuckin' laughin' at me! You think it's funny that me boyfriend's gonna knock me fuckin' head off?"

He held his hands up, a gesture of peace.

"Hey, you can get fingered by whoever you want for me love, I just came out for a good time," he said, "just cool yer jets yeah?"

Long head couldn't get to him in time before she was scooped up from her feet by the strong muscular arms of a bouncer. Her legs flailed. Her arms grappled against the standard black thick material of his coat. The shorter of the two girls wailed after her mate, tugging desperately at the back of the bouncer, earning a mistimed and seemingly accidental elbow to the nose. She fell to the floor dramatically, both hands at her nose, like a continental footballer who'd taken a knock to the chin might do.

"You punched me in me fuckin' nose! You punched me in me fuckin' nose! You fuckin' nobhead!" she sobbed. At this point a variety of lads emerged from the club, the concern they showed toward the girls might have indicated to Jackson that they knew them.

Stepping on the butt of his fag he turned to leave, get back inside away from the impending ruckus.

"What's up Shanice?" said one of the lads, to the long headed girl, now free from the shackles of the bouncer's arms.

"That prick there!" she wailed. Jackson, although he couldn't see who *that prick* might be, had a very good idea.

Beetlejuice

"Come on, let's find Jackson," Beetlejuice suggested to King Smurf, indicating to his brother that the taxi would be due very soon, and his own luck would undoubtedly dictate that if anybody was going to miss it, then Beetlejuice would be that bloke. King Smurf begrudgingly agreed, and the pair circled the club, eyes open for the miserable face of Jackson. He was nowhere to be seen, and it was agreed that if he was anywhere then it would be at the taxi rank, a face like a slapped arse, moaning that he'd had a shit night. They both knew how moody the cunt could be. So they approached the exit, and bemoaned the fact that none of the others had made it to the club that they had all agreed to meet at. A growing noise echoed through the door. Shouting and posturing from men. Screeches of women. The exit opened up as they stepped on to the street to see a single bloke at one end, arms out wide, the universally accepted sign to *bring it on.* Opposite him, beyond the wall of bouncers, were five lads, and a couple of girls, threatening the solitary figure from afar. Beetlejuice was gutted to acknowledge that the solitary figure was Jackson, who'd spotted his mates.

"Dickfingers!" he called, a smile on his face. King Smurf sidled up alongside Jackson, backing up his mate.

"What's up mate?" he said.

"These PRICKS!" said Jackson to King Smurf. Behind the pair was where Beetlejuice had decided to reside, away from the front line but at least in the proximity of his mates so he could quite definitely be construed as showing solidarity, "just trying to have a smoke and them slags start chelpin' at me."

The *slags* heard that, and began their squawking once again.

"Just fuck off yeah?" said a bouncer, his arm pointing off the direction that Beetlejuice *really* wanted to head in, but he knew his brother, and he knew Jackson. Fucking off, they would definitely not be.

"Oi Oi Oi!"

The trio turned to witness an approaching crew, which consisted of Hitler, Superman, and The Incredible Hulk, tailed by three girls. *Thank fuck.*

"Now then boys! Long time no fuckin' see!" laughed Jackson, his back up growing in both size, and fighting ability. Beetlejuice shrunk ever further into the growing throng of heroes.

King Smurf

He knew for a fact that his brother would fanny it. He'd never been known as a fighter, and even when he'd been dragged into things he always came off worse.

"Gav," he said to Beetlejuice, "fuck off yeah?"

The undead prankster nodded a grateful affirmation and stepped slowly away from the gang, each one of them ready to tackle the locals. He took his place alongside the girls that the others had fetched back with them. King Smurf was slightly perturbed to note that all three of them had bigger hands than his brother. He turned back to Jackson.

"What you wanna do pal?"

"See that big cunt there?" Jackson nodded to the one on the end, a mean looking bloke, bigger than the rest, eyeballing them.

"Yeah?"

"Well, I reckon rush that cunt, me and you. These boys can take the others easy."

"You up for that?" asked King Smurf of Hitler, who turned to Superman and Hulk.

"Boys?"

"Fuck it. Let's do it.

***

"We need to get gone if we're gonna get that taxi lads," Dicko says to us, but I know for a fact that Justin's going fucking nowhere, he's smitten by this girly. They're too far gone for fucking. He's stoned as fuck, off his tits on MDMA and affection for what's her name, gently chewing his own lip off and----------------

----

-----------------------------------that boat pub that we
were at earlier on, the lights are on inside but there
are people still floating about, fucking love that pub,
defo coming back there in future. Dicko's trudging
along, looking the dapper motherfucker in the big
purple pimp suit and--

-----where we're going? says Dicko.
"Yeah, for sure, just down----------------------------------

-------------------------the fuck have you boys been?"
says Fingers, his eyes wide as saucers, standing
alongside three trannies, who are actually pretty
convincing, especially the little Oriental dude. My
cock is fucking killing me.
"Off having a little party, a little sexy time, doing a
little of the other. The banjo string snapped, my

friend," I'm saying, pulling his white face toward mine and planting a kiss on his lips, "but the band played on."
He pulls away.
"They've all been arrested or scarpered."
"Who?"
"All of 'em. Jackson got into another fight and they ended up goin' at it with these lads. Where the fuck have youse been?"
He's stressing, but fuck it. It's been a great night. Dicko's looking all confused at these ladyboys----------
----

------the taxi pulls away, and Dicko's slamming his hands on the side of it, screaming blue murder, then he's bringing up their Fiona, saying how she's gonna--
----

--Fingers starts wandering off with the three ladyboys, I wonder if there's gonna be a freaky sexy cockfest going down tonight, and our boy Fingers, the oldest virgin in town, is gonna be the star of the show. Fuck it, each to

their own, every hole's the goal, that's what I say, good luck to him, I've had far too good a night to even let a damaged cock spoil it. I'm not paying for a taxi though, we can go and get some more drinks, make an all-nighter of it, get a train in the morning. Fuck knows where Tony got to. The daft bastard. I'll bet he's not even had *half* as much of a night as us.

Al Capone

"Hey!" said the voice.
Al Capone opened his eyes, slowly. Felt his heavy rock back and forth. The aching reached from the tip of his nose down his neck and into his back. It spread outward through his ribs, into his shoulders, down to the extremities. Eventually it dawned on him that he was seated upright. Arms behind his back. Tied together. A crack of light sliced through the darkness, scattered dust particles, cut into his retina. The shadow moved around behind the crack of light. Capone struggled to make out the shape, until it stepped closer in. Stepped over the threshold of the light, swung a heavy and tight fist into his nose. Capone yelled in pain. The whistles in his head persisted. Subsided.
"Who are you? What do you want?" he said, attempting, and failing, to sound as forceful as he could. He was screwed. The shadow stepped forward again. The taxi driver. Capone's face creased in confusion.
"What? What have I done?"
The driver smiled.
"Boy, you're just havin' a shit night, you just picked the wrong taxi driver to be beggin' from, I'm just gonna give you somethin' to actually beg for."
"What?"

"You know boy? Your life."

Afterword and Acknowledgement

None of these stories were ever intended to help change the world. It's not what I do. They're intended as eleven slices of entertainment. Mostly I want to make you laugh. Maybe make you throw up a little bit in your mouth. Maybe make you cringe. That kind of thing. Not everybody will like what I do, but that's the beauty of this world we live in. We're none of us the same, so if you have words for me, be they kind or otherwise, then please feel free to review my work, or get in touch on Facebook or Twitter. There's literally only one Ryan Bracha on this planet, and it's me, so you'll find me if you want to.

Thank you to my wife, Rebecca. She loves some of the things I do and say, but really she lets a hell of a lot of the things I do and say slide. Let's say she loves me, *despite* the things I do and say.
Thanks to fellow authors Keith Nixon and Mark Wilson. You cats are the reason I figured this mad as fuck industry out, and why I'm still fighting the good fight.

Thanks to Pete Voss, of Campag Velocet. One, for allowing me the use of your lyrics. Two, for being the cool as fuck radge that you are, and providing the world with such quality tunes. Lastly, thanks to the people I never met but who put a great deal of effort into letting me know that what I was doing was hitting home somewhere in the world. You know who you are. It means a lot.

Visit Paddy's Daddy Publishing for more great titles, such as:

<u>Mark Wilson</u>

Paddy's Daddy

Bobby's Boy

Naebody's Hero

Head Boy

<u>Suzanne Egerton</u>

Out Late With Friends and Regrets

<u>Des McAnulty</u>

Life is Local

<u>P.M. Leckie</u>

Stumbledirt

<u>Naebody's Hero</u>
The #1 Bestseller from Mark Wilson, Author of Bobby's Boy

POWER DOESN'T ALWAYS CORRUPT

Abandoned by his parents as a child, Rob Hamilton has developed an unshakeable sense of right and wrong. He also has some very special gifts. If he can stop hiding from them and get his life together he may just be the greatest hero the world will never know.

Arif Ali is an English teenager from Battersea, London who is now living and studying in Pakistan. Arif is about to become a prized asset of Al-Qaeda. He and Rob will form an unlikely friendship that will alter one of the most notorious days in American history.

Kim is an American intelligence agent from Ann Arbor, Michigan. She heads up the agency's anti-terrorist response, is an obsessive workaholic and is relentless in the pursuit of justice. Kim could be the worst enemy the friends have, or their greatest ally.

Set in Scotland, England, Pakistan, Afghanistan, France and the United States; Naebody's Hero is a fast-paced global thriller spanning four decades, reaching its climax on one horrific day in September, 2001.
Inspired by: Suzanne Colins' Hunger Games Trilogy; Kurt Busieks' Secret Identity; Mark Millars' Superman:Red Son and Jonathon Maberrys' Rot and Ruin

17199662R00149

Printed in Poland
by Amazon Fulfillment
Poland Sp. z o.o., Wrocław